FORCED GIGOLOS

FORCED GIGOLOS

ROE RICHMOND

CUTTING EDGE

ISBN-13: 978-1-954840-30-0

Published by
Cutting Edge Books
PO Box 8212
Calabasas, CA 91372
www.cuttingedgebooks.com

PREFACE

Ann Norvill unbuttoned the top two buttons of her blouse and placed Duke Morey's hand up against her well-formed breasts.

"Duke," she said, "this is our last night. I'm a virgin—you know that. But, Duke, I'm not going to see you for ... a long time. Do it, Duke. Take me to bed. I feel like it isn't even me asking you this, Duke. But I know it's all right, because it's *you*. Give me something to make sure that I'll always be yours, Duke. Give me—"

Duke Morey held his woman to him, his hands roving wildly over her buttocks, hips, into the exposed cleavage where her precious bosom was bared for his taking. He opened his big, hard hands wide, slipped them in under her clothing, felt the youngness and eagerness of her exciting body hardening against him, ever so softly shuddering in the beginnings of the passion they had never consummated. The fires rose in Duke Morey and he pushed her down on the couch, pulled the other buttons on her sweater quickly apart, undid the bra that now seemed too small to hold its passionate contents, and pulled the twin prizes to his eager lips. Ann's body jerked close to him, her hands pulling up her skirts 'til it rode high around her waist, her own lips forming the words, "Yes ... yes ... yes ... yes ... yes ..."

Suddenly Duke pulled away. "No," he said.

Ann covered herself, put her hand on his. "Why, Duke?"

"It isn't right, Ann," he said. "Not from any angle. I'm going off to war tomorrow. Neither you or I knows what in the hell will happen. I can't do this to you—with you—much as I want to. When I come home … things will be different. But now—let's just say it this way." Then Duke put his lips gently to Ann's and began buttoning up her sweater again.

CHAPTER ONE

In the bus station on the way there, a busty redhead had stuck her oversized, swelling breasts up against him and smiled out of the corner of her mouth. She wasn't wearing a bra, and her large nipples pushed against the cloth. Duke's first impulse, naturally was to cut the redhead's low cut dress even lower, reach in and free the twin mounds of passion which were his for the asking—or *buying,* anyway. But that was only his first impulse. He thought of Ann and the stacked redhead didn't matter much anymore.

Duke was a man who needed women—in a big way. But right now, and ever since he left her for the Army, all of Duke Morey's dynamic manhood was focused on Ann. Ann of the velvety neck, upthrusting breasts, lean, womanly thighs, passionate but virginal lips.

Duke looked up at the sign.

This was the place all right. He stood on the sidewalk staring at the garish vermilion scroll of neon, CABANA CLUB, framed in flowing poisonous green. It didn't look like much. Just another hole-in-the-wall bar. No place to hold dreams and memories, nothing that a man should long for out in the Pacific. But he had saved it for last because it had been their favorite spot. No sign or word of Ann in all the other haunts. Surely in the Cabana they would know what had become of her, where she had gone. It was a neighborhood bar rather than a tourist trap or a homosexual hangout, such as so many clubs in the Village had become.

Duke Morey crossed the walk to the entrance, a tall rangy young man with a slight hitch in his stride, broad in the shoulders and trim at the waist in well-cut tan gabardine. He paused inside the doorway, as slow, sad piano music floated through the clink of glasses and murmuring voices. Clift was still here, playing one of the old numbers they had liked, hunched and brooding over the keys as if he hadn't moved in two years. Clift would know about Ann Norvill.

The first two bartenders were new and strange, but beyond the elbow at the far end he glimpsed a familiar gleaming bald head and hard broken-nosed profile. Duke Morey moved around the bend and eased into the bar. "Hi, Man."

Manahan's ruddy face lighted. "Duke!" he said, reaching a large knobby hand across the polished wood. "So you're back, boy? And looking like a million." He was already pouring bourbon and soda over cracked ice in a tall glass, about four fingers of whiskey. "On the house, soldier."

"No more, Man. They retired me."

"You're out then? That's good." Manahan sighed and shook his shiny head. "All wars stink but none so much as this one. Like they was playing games with all them rules and peace conferences and that kind of crap. We should care about the politics of South Korea. It don't make sense … But it must've been rough, son."

"Rough enough, Man," said Duke Morey.

"You get shot up?"

"A little. In the left leg. Not bad but I'll never do the hundred in ten seconds again."

"Well, it got you out anyway."

"Yeah, it got me out."

Manahan mopped the bar idly. "Where's Ann, Duke?"

"I was going to ask you that, Man," said Duke Morey dully.

"Haven't seen her in a year, I guess. Heard she'd gone off to get married. Figured it was you, of course."

Duke Morey shook his sandy cropped head. "I haven't heard from her for over a year. And I can't find out a thing about her, Man."

"What about her family, Duke?"

"They live in Cleveland, that's all I know. Ann never said much about them. I think they've got money and she kind of broke with them when she left home." He traced a diamond design with the damp glass.

"Nice girl, Ann," mused Manahan. "But I don't know, Duke… They come and go fast in this town."

"Any of her friends come in here, Man?"

"Not very often. Once in awhile that little dark-haired girl, I can't think of her name."

"Jane Tolman," said Duke Morey. "I can't find her either. It's strange that people can drop out of sight that way. It's got me worried, Man. Something must have happened to Ann."

"Here, lemme freshen that drink up." Manahan splashed more bourbon and soda into the glass, and Duke twirled it slowly in long tanned fingers.

Two men swaggered in, tough-faced and cold-eyed in obviously expensive but poorly tailored suits, padded in the shoulders and tight at the waist and too full in the trousers. They eyed Duke with deliberate insolence and went on to a table. He had seen them around before, and they always gave him that deadpan stare of hostile contempt, for some reason which he couldn't fathom unless it was instinctive dislike of his Anglo-Saxon appearance. The sleek dark one was Italian, and the craggy-faced blond one was probably a Pole. Manahan spoke quietly in response to Duke's questioning look:

"A couple of small-time hoodlums, I think. The Wop's Tony Castelli and the Polack is Franky Borchek. Don't know what their racket is, but they never work and they always have money. Could be they're pimps, they're always chasing the dolls."

"They want something from me," Duke Morey murmured.

3

Manahan grimaced. "They fancy themselves as tough guys, Duke."

"Well, I'll go over and say hello to Clift," said Duke. "Thanks, Man."

"Anybody back from Korea gets a drink here," Manahan said. "And an old friend and customer like you gets as many as he can take, Duke. Lemme give you a refill now and don't pull any money on me either."

Crossing the floor with glass in hand, Duke Morey could feel the eyes of the two hoods on him. He halted and turned to stare steadily back at them, until Castelli's bold swarthy face broke into a sneer and he made some cryptic remark that set Borchek to laughing with him. Duke Morey went on to the piano, and the lackadaisical Clift roused from his reverie to greet Duke with unusual warmth and spirit. But it was discouraging somehow when Clift also inquired for Ann Norvill. It made Duke's search seem more futile and hopeless than ever.

"A man can't afford to lose a gal like Ann," said Clift. "There aren't too many of them left around, Duke."

"I've tried every place I can think of, Clift. I thought sure I'd get a line on her here."

"Sorry, Duke. Wish I could help you, boy. But this place isn't the same any more. No fun like we used to have in here."

"Things change, Clift. Where's La Rose now?"

"She went back to burlesque," Clift said. "You have a stripper in these joints now and you get a houseful of Lesbians. La Rose is a normal healthy gal. She said if she had to dodge passes, she'd rather dodge 'em from men than dames."

They chatted pleasantly about old times and old songs, and Clift ran through a few of their favorites. Glancing back toward the hoodlums, Duke Morey observed that Borchek and Castelli had moved in on a couple of girls in a booth by the wall, and he felt an unreasoning hatred for the two men and disgust for women who would tolerate them. In the dimness the flamboyant blonde sat with crossed legs that exposed an interesting length of silken legs and a few inches of bare white thighs. The brunette seemed more quiet and composed and indifferent, bored by this intrusion.

Tony Castelli, with his large liquid dark eyes and coarse arrogant features and well-greased blue-black curls, might be judged handsome by certain low standards, Duke supposed, and the rough brutal masculinity of the blond Franky Borchek would probably appeal to some girls. But Duke Morey thought that any lady of taste and discrimination, like Ann Norvill, for instance, would find those two characters thoroughly revolting, in looks as well as in their blatant boorish manners.

Duke Morey finally said so long to Clift and started back to the bar to bid Manahan good night, when a vaguely familiar feminine voice startled him by calling his name: "Duke! Duke Morey!" Wheeling toward that booth, he saw that the dark-haired girl was Jane Tolman, and he moved instantly and eagerly forward to grasp her outstretched hand. If anyone would know about Ann Norvill, Jane Tolman certainly should, he thought, forgetful of the blonde and the two men until Tony Castelli's voice rasped jeeringly:

"Blow, brother! On your way, jerk. Nobody wants you here."

Duke Morey looked down at him with icy contempt, seeing the row of gold pens and pencils in Castelli's breast pocket, the gold watch on one thick hairy wrist and the silver bracelet on the other. Jane Tolman started to rise, but Franky Borchek hauled her back into the seat.

"Keep your hands off her," Duke Morey said, teeth on edge. "Let her out of that booth."

Tony Castelli stood up with a sneer, shorter and wider than Duke. "You want trouble, chum, you've got it. Just step out in the alley with me."

Borchek got up too, big and rawboned and ugly, and Duke Morey glanced from one to the other. "You're taking quite a chance. There's only two of you."

"I won't need no help," Castelli said. "I'm taking you myself, mister. If you got guts enough to go out."

Anger flared through Duke Morey. "Come on, then," he said.

"No, Duke, no!" cried Jane Tolman, but Duke Morey was already walking toward the nearby side door that opened into an alley, followed by Castelli and Borchek. At the bar Manahan was busy mixing drinks, and did not see them move outside.

In the murky half-light of the alley, with the sounds of traffic and voices and the smell of gasoline and popcorn coming from the street, Duke Morey turned in time to see Castelli's fist come lashing at him, the knuckles aglint with brass. Ducking, Duke took the crushing metallic impact on his crewcut head as he drove forward. It jarred him to the heels but did not stop him. Sliding in under that arm, Duke Morey sloughed away at the belly with both hands, sinking them deep and solid.

Tony Castelli doubled, his mouth gaping, and Duke Morey hooked him left and right on the loosened jaws, driving him back on the wall, his glossy black head bouncing off the bricks. As Castelli floundered forward on sagging knees, head bowed and arms dangling limp, Duke Morey chopped him wickedly across the back of the neck, beating him face downward in the dirt and ashes.

Duke Morey whirled then to face Franky Borchek but too late, the leather sap was already swishing down on his cropped head. His skull seemed to split open with an explosive roar of flashing light, and the earth rushed up at him as the light dimmed and darkness closed in to drown him deep. Faintly Duke felt the first few jolts of Borcheck's stomping kicking shoes, and then that faded and he felt and saw nothing more.

CHAPTER TWO

D uke Morey came back from a nightmare world to a fragrant comfortable feminine atmosphere that puzzled him. His head throbbed heavily, his eyes focussed poorly, and he groped back in dazed memory to that dim alley outside the Cabana Club and Castelli's dark evil face under his knuckles and the black-jack whipping down in Borchek's hand. But why, why did those hoodlums have the finger on him?...Someone was sitting near the bedside, and Duke murmured, "Ann, Ann."

"No, Duke. It's just Jane Tolman," a soft gentle voice responded. "How's your head feel now? Are you all right?"

"All right," he mumbled, tongue swollen and throat dry. "Little headache is all. Like some water, Jane."

She brought him a cold glass, and pain rocketed through Duke's skull as he raised it off the pillow. No drink, even in combat, had ever tasted better. Duke gulped greedily of the cold soothing water. It eased the crusted dryness of his tongue, the parched ache of his throat. Sunshine was flooding in at the windows. As his vision cleared he saw a clock on the night-stand, its hands upright at twelve o'clock noon.

"I took your bed, Jane," he protested.

"That's all right, Duke. I slept in the other room with Lolly."

"Ann...What's become of Ann, Jane?"

She shook her dark head, lustrous in the sunlight. "Nobody knows, Duke. She—she just disappeared. I wrote her parents. They knew nothing about her and didn't seem interested. Apparently they have more or less disowned her. She left most everything in her studio-apartment, just as it was. I notified the Bureau of Missing Persons, but they haven't turned up anything. Finally I closed up her apartment and stored her belongings. It's been over a year now, and nobody's heard a word from her."

"I knew something was wrong—when she stopped writing," Duke Morey said slowly. "I've got to find her, Jane. We—we were going to be married, when I came back."

"Yes, I know, Duke." Jane Tolman was crying quietly, tears welling from her deep brown eyes and streaming down her softly rounded cheeks. "I—I thought a lot of Ann, too. She was really the best friend I ever had. A wonderful girl, Duke, and she had a lot of talent as a painter, too... I can't understand it at all."

Duke Morey sat up carefully in the soft silken bed, hunched against the pillows, waiting for the drumming pain to slow and diminish in his head. He felt and looked out of place in this dainty feminine bedroom, his long arms emerging brown and muscular from the white T-shirt.

"Don't cry, Jane," he said.

"I—I'm sorry, Duke. Can I get you something to eat or drink?"

"Not right now. Jane, who was Ann seeing before she dropped out of sight? Was she going out with anybody?"

"She didn't go out for a long time after you left, Duke," said Jane Tolman thoughtfully. "Then, a little while before she disappeared, she started going out with a man from Ellinger's Escort Service."

"You mean she—she *paid* for her dates?" Duke's tone and expression were incredulous.

"Ann was lonely, Duke, and she didn't want to get involved with anyone. She had plenty of money to spend, and she thought that was the safest way. It was all impersonal and businesslike with her. She wanted an escort, but she didn't want to become involved with any other man."

"Yeah, I see. But it still sounds screwy, a girl like Ann Norvill."

Jane Tolman nodded. "I'm afraid it was, Duke. I've heard rumors about some of those escort services being fronts for vice rings, kidnappers and blackmailers and white slavers. I—I've been dating some of the boys from Ellinger's myself, trying to get some kind of a line on Ann. They were all perfect gentlemen, but I didn't find out anything."

"What about your friends last night? The brass knuckle and blackjack boys?" Duke Morey inquired, with irony.

"They're no friends of mine, Duke," she said hastily. "Lolly Durand's a good-hearted girl, but she attracts some strange characters. Castelli and Borchek have been after her for a long time."

"What those two meatballs got against me?"

"I don't know, Duke. Unless they were connected with Ann's disappearance, and have learned that you are hunting for her. I wouldn't be surprised if they were in the white-slave trade. Nothing's too low for those two subhuman specimens."

"They look and act the part all right," Duke Morey admitted. "They don't work for that Ellinger outfit, do they?"

"No, Ellinger screens his employees as if he were selecting candidates for the social register," Jane Tolman declared. "His escorts are all courteous intelligent college-bred young men, with perfect manners and beautiful clothes ... I've been thinking, Duke, it might be a good idea for you to get a job there."

Duke Morey laughed. "Me? A gigolo? Come again, Janie!"

"It would be worth it, wouldn't it, if it led you to Ann Norvill?" demanded Jane Tolman.

"Yes, it certainly would," Duke agreed, abruptly sober. "It's about the only lead we've got to work on." He was gradually feeling better and stronger, the ache in his head subsiding and the nausea fading out of his stomach. There was a welted lump on top of his crew-cut head, but it didn't seem to be anything serious.

"Ellinger was advertising for help a while ago," Jane said. "I've got the clippings somewhere. You'd fit the bill to perfection, Duke."

Duke Morey grinned boyishly at her. "That's a very dubious compliment, young lady."

"I meant it as a real compliment, Duke. They want them tall, handsome, well-dressed and well-mannered."

"I might take a fling at it, Jane," he said. "Wonder how you'd go about it?"

"There's a nice bar called the Rendezvous, right across the street from the Ellinger building, which resembles an exclusive club for young men. If I were you I'd hang around the Rendezvous and get acquainted with some of Ellinger's glamor boys. Sort of let them talk you into applying for a job."

"Well, I've got to do something pretty soon," Duke Morey confessed. "The money I saved in the Army isn't going to last forever. First time I ever saved any dough, simply because there was nothing to spend it on. Except gambling, and I happened to have a good run with the dice and cards." He shook his sandy head sorrowfully. "Had enough to get married on, in a modest way, but the bride is missing."

"Perhaps we'll find her, Duke, now that you're back," Jane said. "I feel a great deal better to have you here anyway ... If you want to shave and shower now, you'll find everything in the bathroom. And then we'll have some lunch—or breakfast."

"You're awful good to me, Janie," he said, smiling at her.

"The modern Edith Cavell," she said, rising with easy grace and walking from the room, small but exquisitely formed and fully rounded, a dark vivid little girl in casually smart clothes. Duke remembered that Jane Tolman wrote poetry, lived on an ample allowance from her well-to-do family in Michigan, and sometimes worked in advertising. A frank, straightforward, sincere young woman, without pretense or artifice. Duke had always liked her, even when he was most engrossed in Ann Norvill, and they always got along fine together.

In the bathroom Jane had laid out shaving equipment and a new toothbrush for him, and his tan gabardine suit was hanging there all cleaned and pressed. Duke Morey felt much better after shaving and brushing his teeth, and the showerbath soothed and revived him. Glowing clean and immaculate in the gabardine, he emerged to find the bright brassy blonde, Lolly Durand, chattering away there to Jane Tolman.

Regarding him with bold approval, as Jane introduced them, Lolly said: "Hm-mm, I see what you mean about him being worth saving, Jane." She was a frivolous flighty girl, with full-blown exaggerated curves at breast and hip, and an avid burning interest in all mankind, that was obvious in her large blue eyes and fluttering mannerisms. "I don't know what got into Tony and Franky last night," Lolly Durand went on. "They must of been drunk or coked-up or something. I'm awfully sorry they picked on you—Duke."

"I wasn't doing bad until Franky came up with a blackjack," Duke Morey said, grinning. "How'd you girls get me up here anyway?"

"Manahan called a cab and came along to help the driver get you upstairs," Jane Tolman said. "It's a good thing Castelli and Borchek beat it, because Manny was ready to kill them both."

"Manny better not get tough with them two," Lolly Durand said. "They'll wrap that joint right around his ears!"

"Rough boys, huh?" murmured Duke Morey. "Two on one, you wouldn't think they'd need brass knucks and a sap."

"They're strictly no-good scum," Jane Tolman said. "You keep fooling around wtih them, Lolly, and you'll find out what they really are."

Lolly Durand giggled and hugged her high full breasts. "They're exciting, Jane. I love men to be wild and exciting and brutal like!"

"You'll get more excitement and brutality than you bargain for, one of these nights," warned Jane Tolman.

Lunch was quite pleasant in the apartment, in spite of Lolly's silly cackling about boy-friends and clothes, movie stars and dance bands. Jane Tolman cooked and kept house as well as she did almost everything, and Duke Morey remarked that somebody was sure missing out on a good wife here.

"I know it," Lolly Durand said. "Jane's so good at everything, and I'm good for nothing but loving." She rolled her prominent eyes and squirmed rapturously in her chair. "But I'll bet some sucker marries me before anybody gets smart enough to marry Jane."

"You may not be so good at loving as you think, Lolly," needled Duke. "They say the mild quiet ones are really better than the loud brazen type."

Lolly eyed him with challenging scorn. "Well, I never had no complaints yet, Mr. Morey!" she declared. "I imagine I could teach you a few things about loving, too!"

"No doubt about that," Duke said easily. "I'm still an innocent naive country boy at heart."

"I guess you probably been around enough," Lolly conceded. "But I never saw the guy yet I couldn't handle. Maybe I'm not smart in books and stuff like that, but when it comes to sex I'm right on the ball, brother. And don't you forget it!"

"I can well believe it, Lolly," said Duke. "Don't get excited, I was only kidding."

"I don't like to be kidded about the one thing I'm best at," Lolly said sulkily.

"I didn't realize your art meant so much to you, Lolly."

She tossed her blonde head and glared at him. "It *is* an art too, just as much as painting pictures or making statues or writing books!"

"It certainly is," agreed Duke Morey. "The most fundamental art of all, Lolly."

"What we fighting about then, Duke?" she pouted. "I don't want to fight with any old friend of Jane's—and Ann Norvill's."

"We aren't fighting, baby. So you know Ann, too?"

"I sure do," Lolly Durand said. "The nicest sweetest girl in the world. Next to Jane, I mean ... I've sure been lucky to have two friends like Ann and Jane."

After Lolly had returned to work in her department store, Duke Morey glanced gravely at Jane. "How do you stand that all the time?"

"Sometimes I wonder, Duke," confessed Jane Tolman. "But Lolly really isn't as bad as she sounds. She's simple and gaudy, but she's also generous and loyal, and sometimes she's good company. I—I've been lonely, since Ann went away, you know. And Lolly pays half the rent and the grocery bill, to put it in a practical way."

"No men in your life, Jane?"

"Not at present, Duke. None that count anyway."

"Well, I could be a big brother to you."

"You always were," she said, smiling up at him from the kitchen sink, as he dried the dishes for her with scrupulous care.

"Let's go to the ball game this afternoon, Jane," suggested Duke Morey. "I'm getting tired of going out there alone."

"Sounds good, Duke. Cleveland's in town, aren't they? I haven't seen a game all season."

They went out to the Stadium and watched the Indians beat the Yankees in a tight 3-2 pitching duel.

Duke took her to dinner at the Roosevelt grill, and they danced to some sweet music. Jane bit her lip and pulled away a little when Duke's thighs accidentally pushed up too close to hers once. When they parted that night, he said he was going to try Ellinger's escort service, and Jane Tolman rummaged through her bag and handed him the advertisement she'd clipped from the paper. He bent down to give her a brotherly kiss then, but her breasts rubbed against him and she flushed and quickly pulled back, saying *goodnight*. Once inside, she undressed to bra and panties, dropped down upon the bed. She lay there, her eyes closed, her lips opening and closing. Her breath came in tiny gasps. "Duke ..." she whispered to herself. "Duke ..." Her hands went to her back, unhooked the bra. She slid her hands in under it, cupped her breasts, moving them back and forth until the tips became hard and hurting. "No, I mustn't!" she half-moaned to herself, pulling her hands from her young, pulsating bosom. She lay there for a minute, her legs moving slowly from side to side, her hands quiet. Then she whispered, "Oh, I can't help it, I can't help it ..." and put her fingers to her mouth, running her wet tongue over them. Then she grasped the tips of her breasts once more, rubbing violently, frantically. "Oh, Duke," she moaned, "Duke ..." as she reached down awkwardly with one hand and pulled off her panties. "Duke ... Duke ..." she moaned. "Oh, Duke honey, Duke man, Duke da-a-a-a-aaady ..."

Back in his hotel room, Duke Morey lay awake a long time listening to the late-night street sounds and watching the colored lights streak and shift on the ceiling and thinking of Ann Norvill. He could see her proud rich chestnut head and deep blue eyes, the fine classic features that were saved from austerity by the slightly tilted nose and the broad fullness of the mouth, the flowing curves and grace of her lithe streamlined figure. He could hear her low husky voice and her delightful lilting laughter, and feel again the strong surge of emotional hunger she never failed to stir and arouse in him.

Duke Morey wanted her back, needed her as he had never needed anything else. He had to find Ann. That was it. But Duke was a man, a big man, and he needed something else, too. He couldn't help thinking of Jane for a minute, how she'd flushed when her heavy, erect breasts met his. She might have that volcano of passion in her that Duke went for in a woman—that he'd gone for in Ann. A volcano—ice covered. He wondered for a moment what Jane was doing right now.

CHAPTER THREE

Three days later in his room, Duke Morey shaved and bathed and dressed in a freshly cleaned and pressed gray summer-weight suit, with particular thoroughness. This might be the day, he thought. He had been hanging around the Rendezvous, and had struck up a speaking acquaintance with several smartly-groomed young men from Ellinger's Escort Service. Duke had let it be known that he was drifting around at loose ends, running out of funds after being discharged from the Army, and not averse to making a few quick bucks if the opportunity arose.

He glanced again at the crumpled notice Jane Tolman had clipped from the Help Wanted ads:

YOUNG MEN: 22-36, educated, cultured, sophisticated. Attractive, well-dressed, personable. Entertaining companions and good dancers preferred. Must be gentlemen, familiar with the city amusement places, hotels, restaurants, night clubs, etc. At home in all strata of society ...

They don't want much for escorts nowadays, Duke Morey thought, with a wry grin. Nothing but big leaguers ... Half-humorously he checked himself against the requirements specified in Ellinger's advertisement. Within the age bracket at twenty-six, and he had a B.A. from Wisconsin (for baseball and basketball, his dad used to say, a B.A.B. degree). A little low on culture maybe, but sophisticated enough to get by in most circles. No screen star, but fairly good-looking in a big clean casual way, with a rangy, wide-shouldered, slim-waisted build that made clothes look better tailored than they actually were.

He could be entertaining, if they didn't demand too much romantic charm, and he could dance acceptably, if they didn't go in for the fast, fancy stuff. The spots around town were known to him, and he had mingled in most all levels of society... Yes, Duke Morey concluded, I ought to pass all right. Not magna cum laude, but with about a B average.

Before the full-length mirror in the bathroom door, Duke adjusted the perfect knot of his narrow striped tie in the round tabbed collar, inspected the easy drape of the handsome gray suit, and left the hotel room, humming *Just a Gigolo*, with ironical amusement.

The Rendezvous was a comfortable masculine bar, not too smart or modern, the juke box blaring but seldom, the television screen utilized mainly for sports events. Across the way was the severe brownstone building of Ellinger's Escort Service, which had the appearance of being a fashionable club for young men, as Jane had told him.

Duke Morey nursed his bourbon-and-soda at the bar, aware of the presence of one of Ellinger's elegant young men, who was even taller than Duke's six-two height and broader of shoulder, grave and distinguished in a flawlessly tailored tropical suit. He had crisp brown hair, strange amber eyes, and a manner of easy assurance. Nodding and smiling at Duke over his glass, the young man moved over and slid onto the next stool.

"Seen you around. My name's Tom Garrick."

Duke Morey shook hands and gave his own name. They chatted carelessly about the weather, baseball, politics, and bought each other drinks, and Garrick finally asked Duke if he was employed at the moment, or one of the idle rich. Duke said he was neither, just shopping around, and Garrick surveyed him with critical approval.

"You'd do all right in our racket, Morey," said Tom Garrick, and when Duke looked questioningly at him, he went on to explain the business of providing escorts for lonely women in the great city. Ellinger had built it into something really big time, Garrick declared. Ellinger knew everybody and had friends and ins and strings to pull everywhere. That, and discreet advertising in the best women's hotel's, clubs, schools, apartment and rooming houses, attracted so many clients that the agency could afford to be discriminating. The older ladies, the less appealing and less wealthy, were tactfully sidetracked to other escort bureaus, whenever possible.

"I know how you feel, Morey," said Tom Garrick. "There's a natural prejudice against this type of thing. I had it myself in the beginning. But frankly, I don't know where else I could make a couple or three hundred a week, and enjoy myself while doing it."

"Do you make that much?" Duke asked, in genuine surprise.

"Not at first, of course. But after you get started you do, and sometimes a lot more. The tips are amazing."

"But don't you feel like a heel?"

Garrick laughed. "You get over that, too. Women with a lot of money are going to throw it around anyway. If you don't get it somebody else will, and it's never enough to hurt them ... We render other services too, escorting young girls without much money but with a lot of beauty and charm. We have started careers for many of them, in radio and television and show business. Some of our clients end up on Broadway or in Hollywood."

Duke Morey nodded somberly, thinking: *Yes, but a lot more of them probably end up in brothels and asylums, in the river or on a slab in the morgue* ... But he knew it was unfair to think these thoughts without any evidence, prompted by nothing but suspicion because Ann Norvill and other young girls had vanished from the heart of the city.

"You still don't like it?" Tom Garrick said.

"Not very well," admitted Duke Morey. "But I'm getting low in funds. I've got to do something pretty soon."

"Better think it over, Morey," advised Garrick. "There aren't too many ten-thousand-a-year or better jobs open. Especially jobs in which you have fun and wine and dine on the best, while earning your salary."

"Only too true," agreed Duke, thinking of his pittance in the Army, and what he had gone through for it.

Tom Garrick was interrupted then by the arrival of two compatriots, whom he introduced to Duke with an expression that seemed to say, *Please don't judge us all by these two*... Payton Frappier, foppish and dapper, overdressed, marcelled and scented, had long-lashed violet eyes and full insolent lips under a neat mustache. Clyde Vorse was short, stocky and compact, with a refined intellectual face, cold superior eyes, and a stern almost cruel mouth under a sharp predatory nose. They greeted Duke without enthusiasm, but evinced some interest when they learned he was thinking of joining the House of Ellinger.

Payton Frappier immediately sketched a fanciful picture of the sensuous delights accompanying their duties. Clyde Vorse said, with cool irony: "Don't let Frap mislead you, Morey. It can be pleasant, at times, but it's far from paradise. Seduction is not our practice, although we are sometimes hard put to avoid being seduced ourselves."

"You can say that again!" Frappier said, with feeling. "The other night I drew a babe that was full of some kind of aphrodisiac. What an experience! It must have been undiluted Spanish fly. I've never seen anything so hot. She was in a veritable frenzy, and the things that girl wanted to do! Honest to God, I thought I'd never get out of her room intact and alive!"

Slightly sickened by Frappier, Duke Morey listened to some further discussion and finally allowed himself to be persuaded to cross the street for an interview with Horace Ellinger, director of the organization, which Garrick arranged by telephone.

Duke acted reluctant and doubtful throughout, while inwardly congratulating himself on the way things were breaking. This might be another dead end, but it was worth trying. Someone in this agency had been out with Ann Norvill shortly before she disappeared from the face of the earth.

The interior of the brownstone building was furnished with great luxury and excellent taste, resembling more than ever an exclusive and expensive club. There was a large lobby, spacious comfortable lounges, an extensive library, card and game rooms with billiard, pool and pingpong tables, and a television theater. There was a big main dining hall, as well as small private dining rooms, and a richly-stocked and elaborate bar. In the basement were bowling alleys, a gymnasium, and a swimming pool. The upper floors were devoted to bedrooms and baths, occupied by the young gentlemen, who were all required to live within the building. No hardship, to be sure, yet Duke wondered about that ruling.

In a bare bleak private office, contrasting oddly with the general elegance, Duke Morey was presented to Horace Ellinger, a small plump man with a thick neck and oversized bristly head. Squatting in his chair, Ellinger wore horn-rimmed glasses that made his eyes appear bulbous and froglike. His broad bloated face was lividly pale, beneath a blue-black beard that resisted the closest shaving. On the desk his hands were incongruously slender and patrician, except for the black hair curling on their backs. His dark suit looked rusty and rumpled, as if he had slept in it. Horace Ellinger would never have answered one of his own ads.

He gave Duke Morey some blanks to fill out, and studied him as he wrote answers into the detailed questionnaires. He asked for identification, which Duke produced in the form of Army discharge, driver's license, social security card, club and fraternal memberships. Then, with the filled forms in hand, Ellinger asked brief pertinent questions. Did Morey like women, get along well with them? Was he highly, average, or under sexed? Had he ever been in trouble with girls? Was he bitter after his military experiences in Korea? Could he do this kind of work and retain his self-respect? ... At the close of the interview, Ellinger gave no indication of his reaction to Duke Morey. He simply said:

"That's all. I will check your references, and inform you of our decision in due time."

Relieved when the curt dismissal came, Duke realized that Horace Ellinger was a thoroughly formidable person, an extraordinary man to be engaged in such an enterprise. Unless it did go deeper than the surface revealed ... In the outer office he met two men, who introduced themselves as Mr. Ellinger's associates and shook hands with Duke.

Neither of them would have filled the requirements specified in Ellinger's advertisement. Ben Zolnay was broad and squat, beak-faced with an ugly jutting jaw and a brutal clipped head. Rufus Kern, long, lean and lanky, had a narrow hatchet-face under a wiry brush of reddish hair.

Their cold, calculating, utterly ruthless appearance tempted Duke Morey to think he might be on the right trail after all. Zolnay and Kern looked like men who would stop at nothing, to further their own interests. They had the opaque inhuman eyes and calm expressionless faces of professional killers, he thought.

Back with Tom Garrick, Duke Morey wandered about the strange establishment, trying to shake off a persistent sense of unreality.

"How'd it go, Morey?" asked Garrick cheerfully.

Duke grinned. "I don't think the big boss was exactly overwhelmed."

"He never is," Garrick laughed. "It'd take something way out of this world to overwhelm Horace Ellinger. But he is considering you seriously, or he wouldn't have wasted that much time on you."

"I don't know whether that's good or bad."

"You'll find this isn't a bad life—if you get in," Garrick said. "It's like being back at school, without any classes to go to. There's a good bunch of fellows around, along with the usual jerks, and you can see that we live in luxury here."

"It's a nice layout all right," Duke conceded. "But don't you ever feel like a prisoner, Garrick?"

"Sometimes, perhaps," Tom Garrick confessed. "But in general we have plenty of freedom."

"Did you ever meet up with a girl named Ann Norvill?"

Garrick pondered over the name, and shook his crisp brown head. "Not that I remember. We meet so many, of course, it's impossible to remember them all."

"You wouldn't forget her," Duke Morey said.

"If she's that good I probably wouldn't," Garrick said. "Must be I never met her, Morey."

In the lobby, Duke was introduced to some more of the young men, most of whom seemed to be the nice-looking clean-cut types, common to any American campus. Bill Howell, big, rugged and good-natured, had been a football star at Cornell, and Sid Pawley was a socialite from Princeton ... Gene Desmond was tall and strong, beautifully built and well coordinated, strikingly handsome with black hair and very blue eyes and a charming smile. Park Lomax, slender and blond with pale narrow eyes and a shy grin, was soft-spoken and quiet, but Duke thought there was something dangerous, tough and menacing, under his mild exterior manner ... Rudy Valance was suave and polished and worldly wise. And there was Spider Pratt, the small warped and wizened handy man of the household, a favorite with all the boys.

At Garrick's suggestion they took a swim in the pool downstairs, and Duke found the water just right and the springboards excellent. Immeasurably refreshed, he decided this wouldn't be such a bad place to live, at that. As they were leisurely getting dressed, Tom Garrick said:

"Have dinner with me, Morey, and I'll tell you more about being rented out by the day or night to glamorize life for lonely and forlorn maidens, matrons, and even matriarchs, now and then."

Duke agreed readily, thinking that the quicker he learned the better.

Garrick consulted a fine platinum wristwatch. "Yes, I have time. Before I go to answer a repeat call from the misunderstood cattle heiress from Helena, Montana." He tapped the watch. "This was a present, Morey, from a satisfied and appreciative customer from New Orleans..."

When Duke Morey got back to his hotel room that night, everything seemed to be in order, yet he could tell it had been thoroughly ransacked and searched by experts.

He wasn't too surprised, except by the suddenness of it. They could have found nothing but what corroborated his harmless identity as Darnell Duke Morey, lately of the U. S. Army. There wasn't even a gun among his innocuous belongings.

Duke was rather pleased, because it indicated that he might be on the track of something subversive, which might in time lead him to Ann Norvill.

CHAPTER FOUR

While waiting to hear from Ellinger, Duke Morey took out Jane Tolman. "I've got to get in practice, Janie," he explained. "Those gook women in Korea didn't appeal much to me, and I wasn't in Japan long enough for the geisha girls to look very white. Although some of them were quite pretty." It was easy enough to pretend flippancy, but Duke Morey was haunted by memories that would give him a bad time the rest of his life. In the ghastly retreat from Chang-jin Reservoir, his company had been almost wiped out, only seventeen men out of 132 finally reaching Hungnam, the rest either killed or wounded or missing in the frozen wastelands.

Duke and Jane had a good time together, loafing in Washington Square and drinking in the Cabana Club and other Village bars, but always they were searching for some sign of Ann Norvill.

They even followed the tourists to Radio City and the Empire State tower and Grant's Tomb, and made an excursion to the Statue of Liberty, and rode the ferry to Staten Island and Jersey. They wandered through Wall Street, and window-shopped along Fifth and Park Avenue, and nursed drinks and watched lovers meet in the Astor bar. It was fun, but the ghost of Ann Norvill was always with them, all the way from the Waldorf to McSorley's Saloon.

It was a pleasant interlude, yet Duke Morey had a sense of time wasting and running out to no avail, of Ann hurt and helpless somewhere, held captive and waiting for him to come and rescue her. Either that or dead ... It was Jane Tolman who first admitted that she feared Ann Norvill was dead.

"I have dreams, Duke, and I can see her dead," Jane said brokenly. "If—if she was alive, she'd write or get word to us somehow."

Duke had those dreams too, but he refused to believe them or give Ann up as dead. Something had happened to her, something bad, but he was sure she was still alive, alive and in need of his help ... No other girl had ever mattered like this to Duke Morey, and he felt that none ever would. Ann Norvill was the one, and he had to find her.

Jane Tolman was also worried about Lolly Durand. "She's still going out with that awful Castelli and Borchek, I don't know why. Lolly's simple but she's straight and clean and decent. All that sex chatter is bravado, on her part. She wants to act sophisticated, and she isn't, Duke. She's really a nice innocent kid."

"She won't be long, if she keeps playing tag with those two punks," Duke Morey said. "But you aren't her mother or her sister, Jane. You can't live her life for her."

"I'm her friend," Jane Tolman said. "I don't want to see her throw herself away on those two animals."

Duke shrugged. "Well, she seems determined on it. How you going to stop her?" When Jane gestured despairingly, he went on: "It's not as if she was a teen-age virgin."

"She's twenty-two," Jane said. "But I—I think she's still a virgin, Duke."

He laughed quietly. "She sure tries to conceal that fact then."

"That's what makes it so pathetic," Jane Tolman murmured.

"I can't cry for her, Janie," said Duke Morey. "The world's full of girls like her, flirting around and asking for trouble. Sooner or later they get it. So what? After the first time they either learn something and grow up and straighten out, or they keep rolling over for every guy that comes along."

"Men are selfish and heartless."

"It's a hard heartless world, Janie," said Duke. "And women have done their share toward making it that way."

"But what'll become of poor Lolly Durand?"

"From where I sit I see two possible courses for her," Duke said. "With luck she might get to be a fifty or a hundred dollar call girl. Without it, she'll probably wind up in a five-buck bordello."

"Don't be so bitter and cruel, Duke!"

Duke Morey grinned crookedly. "I can't bleed for all the prostitutes and potentials in this fair land of ours, Jane."

"I suppose you're sensible and right," Jane Tolman said. "But I hate to see Lolly go that way..."

Most of the time, however, Jane was a gay charming companion, sweet and lovable, and now and then Duke Morey hungered for her, in spite of his brooding preoccupation with Ann Norvill. On her part, Jane had always liked Duke and secretly envied Ann her hold on him.

But Ann was always there in their minds, and it kept their relationship on a cool friendly basis—for the most part.

"Do you think I'll be a success as an escort?" laughed Duke Morey. "Providing I get the job, that is."

"You're bound to, Duke, you can't miss," declared Jane. "And after you start work I suppose I'll have to pay for the privilege of seeing you. It's a good thing I get a generous allowance from home."

He shook his close-cropped head. "I still can't see myself squiring a lot of strange screwball dames around town and spending their money."

"Why, you'll probably love every minute of it, Duke! You'll think you never had it so good."

"I doubt it, Janie," said Duke Morey seriously. I couldn't do it if it wasn't for trying to get a trace of Ann."

"How did Ellinger's strike you, Duke? You haven't said much about it."

"It seemed to be on the level, but it's too early to tell. Most of the young men appear to be the kind you'd meet at any good university, but Ellinger himself and Zolnay and Kern might be almost anything. I like Tom Garrick pretty well, and he said he'd arrange to room with me, if I make the grade there."

"You'll make it all right, Duke."

"I don't know, Jane," he said. "It's taking them a long while to decide. They must check a guy very thoroughly."

"I told you they did," Jane Tolman reminded him. "You've got to be a thoroughbred to get into Ellinger's stud book."

Duke Morey laughed and shook a reproving finger at her. "Don't get vulgar, little girl."

"I'm not vulgar, just truthful," said Jane Tolman, smiling.

One night Jane looked particularly smart, lovely and desirable, in a tailored rust-brown suit, and Duke drank a little more than usual, in an effort to submerge his craving for her. Back in the apartment Lolly Durand wasn't home yet, and Jane asked him to stay awhile, but Duke Morey shook his high tawny head. "No, I'd better turn in. Might get my call to arms tomorrow, Janie."

She walked toward him, dark head tilted back, eyes and face grave and intent, the clean line of her lifted chin and throat pure and breathtaking. Her fragrance filled his head, and her lips were lushly ripe, parted slightly on white even teeth. He was all too aware of her vibrant nearness, the full curved depths of her body at breast and hip. Suddenly it was as if something flared up between them, and a shocking current drew them together in a fierce hard-locked embrace, their arms gripping, their mouths crushed and clinging.

It seemed to happen without volition on either side, naturally and inevitably. Neither of them had wanted it, but there it was, deeper, stronger than both of them. Jane's mouth opened under his, the pressure of her breasts and opening thighs increased under him, and sharp, unbearable passion surged through him until Jane could feel it, thrillingly. They were both lost, then.

Duke's hands went up to Jane's chest, rubbed softly but urgently against the underside of her breasts. She took his hands, placed them down on her hips, whispered, gasping, "Wait…" Then her hands went to her back, slid under the blouse, undid her bra. Quickly she shrugged out of her suit coat, unbuttoned her blouse and started to let it fall from her shoulders, the bra with it. When Duke got his first glimpse of her full, bulging bosom, he moved his hands down and behind her, around her lush buttocks, pulling her to him hard, his lips buried in her neck, kissing here, there, faster, faster. Her hands went to his head, circling around it, as she pulled it down to her exposed breasts. He pushed her back onto the couch, his mouth wildly caressing her breasts, her young, virgin nipples responding fiercely to the harshly exciting stubble of his beard, the insistent tug of his lips, the unbearable probe of his tongue, the brutal, organiastic brush of his teeth. Her hands dug into his head, the nails scraping the scalp through the short crew cut, drawing little trickles of blood. "Duke," she gasped, her thighs straining to make contact with some part of him, when the door opened.

He put her down, breathless and shaken, quickly picked up her blouse and threw it around her. She buttoned it quickly, stuffing the bra in the pocket of her suit coat, as Lolly Durand sagged against the doorway, a silly grin on her lipstick-smeared face. Her yellow hair was tumbled in wild disarray, and her blue eyes were bulging, dilated and strongly glazed.

"Don't let me stop you, folks," giggled Lolly Durand. "Go right ahead with it. You only live once, and not very long at that…"

Duke Morey strode toward her. Even through the whiskey he had drunk, he caught the reek of liquor and some other rank smell from her. Marihuana, unmistakably raw on her breath, and that glassy drugged look in her eyes.

"So, they've got you on reefers now," Duke Morey said. "Next thing you'll be taking the needle, and then you'll wind up in

Bellevue. Or some cheap whorehouse." He stepped past her into the hall, and slammed the door shut behind him.

Franky Borchek looked back from the head of the stairs, the faint yellow light flickering on his shaggy blond head and rough ugly features. Tony Castelli was not in sight. "Hey, you," Duke said, and walked forward in the dim corridor. Borchek turned and waited, his face impassive and rocklike.

"Start reaching for your blackjack, boy," said Duke Morey.

"I don't need it, chum," Franky Borchek said, his huge heavy-boned hands coming up into fists. "You're a hog for punishment, feller."

"Where's your partner?"

"I don't need him neither. Come and get it, punk."

"What's the idea of feeding that girl marihuana?"

"She wanted it," Borchek said. "You ain't her guardian no more'n I am. Women that go out with me get what they want and plenty of it, brother!"

They came together swinging savagely, and Duke Morey took a couple of roundhouse clouts on the sides of his head, heavy and jolting. Then Duke was inside those wide flailing arms, ripping straight lefts and rights into that craggy face, the solid impacts rippling up his arms. Franky Borchek's head rocked far back, and he reeled off balance against the banister at the stairhead. Duke Morey struck again with shattering force, left and right, blood spraying under his knuckles and that shag-head bobbing violently.

Borchek lunged forward off the rail with hands low, snarling curses and blowing blood. He ran straight into a lashing left that stiffened him up tall and set him back on his heels. Duke Morey let go with another left, and poured all his hundred-and-ninety pounds into a whipping right hand. It landed with a sodden chopping smash, and Franky Borchek fell backward and down the stairway, tumbling heels over head, sprawling and rolling finally to a stop about twenty steps down.

Duke Morey stood watching him, panting hard and mas-
saging his sore knuckles. Something moved at the bottom of
the stairs. Tony Castelli, squaring off in a crouch, his right hand
rising with the glimmer of blued steel in it. Duke dodged back
as flame blossomed from that hand with a crashing roar, and a
bullet tore splinters from the handrail at the head of the stairway and loosed a filtering rain of mortar from the ceiling of the
corridor.

Franky Borchek was up now, blundering and stumbling
down toward the foot of the stairs, and Duke heard his hoarse
growling voice: "Put up that rod, you crazy bastard, and get the
hell outa here!" Then they were gone, and doors were opening all
along the hallway, with anxious curious heads thrusting out and
wide eyes fixed on Duke.

"It's all right, it's nothing," Duke Morey told them, walking
back to Jane's apartment. "Just some drunk shooting off blanks,
I guess."

Lolly Durand had passed out and Jane Tolman was putting her
to bed, and Duke inadvertently got a glimpse of long bare legs and
naked golden breasts, before turning away to pour himself a drink
from the bottle of brandy Jane kept on hand. He needed the reassuring lift and warmth of that one. Those two hoodlums played
rough and for keeps. Sooner or later, Duke thought, I'll have to kill
those two boys, before they get a chance to knock me off.

"What happened out there, Duke?" called Jane. "Did somebody fire a shot?"

"Yeah, one of Lolly's little playmates, hopped to the eyes,"
Duke Morey said. "I knocked Borchek downstairs, and Castelli
took a shot at me from the bottom. Didn't even come close
though. Nothing to worry about."

Jane Tolman came out of the bedroom. "You'd better stay
here tonight, Duke. They may be waiting outside for you."

"No, they scrammed, Jane. They won't be hanging around
here. I'll be okay, baby."

"Isn't it awful to get mixed up with characters like that?" Jane sighed. "Damn that empty-headed Lolly! I knew something like this would happen, if she didn't break away from Borchek and Castelli."

"That's the way they work, Janie," said Duke grimly. "First liquor and reefers, then the real dope. And then the gal wakes up in what they used to call a house of ill fame."

"I wish you'd stay, Duke."

"No, I'd better go, Jane." He kissed her good night, with cool brotherly restraint this time, hard as it was for him. You don't start something with a chick when her roomie is in the next room. Besides, Duke was thinking of Ann again.

When the door closed, Jane leaned against the hard, cool wall next to it. She looked down at her blouse. The dark tips of her breasts shown through the light nylon, still hard, erect, waiting. She closed her eyes hard and thought of it for a moment. "Oh, god," she whispered to herself. "What'll I do? What'll I do?" Her body pressed against the door, the hard doorknob hitting against her upper thighs until she had to bite her lip in pain. She ran into the bathroom and locked the door, undressed quickly and threw herself under a cold shower. The water only seemed to make her more aware of the heat inside her. She stepped out of the shower without turning it off and pounded her fists hard against the sink. "Oh, what'll I do?" she moaned. Her hands went to her own body then, frantically rubbing every inch of it, as if those hands were Duke's, but somehow that didn't help. Tonight it had to be the real thing or nothing. She unlocked the door, rushed to her closet and threw on a robe. Then she ran to the front door and flung it open. "Duke!" she cried out. He was gone. Her impulse was to run out in the street, try and catch him before he was out of sight, but her common sense got the best of her and she closed the door. No amount of sense would ease the aching in her loins, however. She hurried back into the bathroom, noticing Lolly sleeping soundly on the way, and locked the door behind her again. She got out the polish to do her nails, but knew that it was no go. The pleasure-pain within her was getting worse. She unlocked the door once more, rushed to the phone, dialed Duke's number. The hotel said he wasn't in. Now she didn't know what to do. She went into the bathroom again, almost in tears, her body aching hard now. "Oh, why have I always been so over-sexed," she moaned. "Why can't I just…" Talk was no good. She couldn't convince herself out of this feeling. She looked in the mirror. Her breasts were swollen with desire, her lips hard and red with blood welling up in them, her cheeks flushed. "Oh, oh, what can I do?" she said over and over. She stepped back into the shower, turned the water to a little warmer. "I'll wash," she said to herself half aloud, hardly able to get the words out, her breath was coming in such quick gasps. "I'll make myself clean, yes, that's what I'll do, I'll wash off this feeling from my body…" She picked up the soap and rubbed it on her arms and shoulders, then her heaving bosom. "I'll wash this feeling away from my breasts, I'll make it go away by washing it away," she repeated to herself, as her hands moved fluidly over her soapcovered bosom, first slowly, then more quickly. "I'll wash this feeling away," she moaned, as the passion, like a thousand flames, welled up higher and higher in her. "Now here," she said, moving her hands from her bosom. "I'll wash it away, I'll wash it away from *here*, I'll wash it away," she whispered, gasping for breath. She didn't even real-ize what she was doing until the soap dropped from her uncon-trollably shuddering hand. "Oh," she cried, "what a girl has to do to stay a virgin! Ohhh…"

Duke arrived at the hotel with a message waiting for him. It was from Horace Ellinger, and it instructed him to report for employment at his earliest convenience. Duke smiled. Things were going o.k.

One thing still bothered him, though—besides Ann. It was the unfinished business with Jane. Duke knew he had to have a woman. But it couldn't be Jane. She was pure—no doubt about it.

And if Lolly hadn't walked in when she did, he might've spoiled that. He was glad he didn't—although he knew if he were in the same room with the voluptuous Jane now, he would rape her. "I've got to get something, and quick," he muttered to himself, walking out of the hotel.

He found a little bar on Peale street, with a little blonde in it. Her body was full even though she seemed young, and he had no trouble picking her up and taking her back to the hotel. Once there, he didn't wait. He hated pickups, he hated himself for resorting to one, but what could he do? At least he hadn't tarnished Jane. He almost tore the clothes off the girl as he went for her. After he'd somewhat exhausted himself with the third conquest, he reached in his wallet for a twenty and handed it to her. "Thanks, baby," he said. "Now get out."

CHAPTER FIVE

Duke Morey checked out of the hotel and moved into a large comfortable double-room with Tom Garrick in the Ellinger building. It was handsomely furnished, light and pleasant and cool in the summer heat. They had a three-quarter bed, closet, chest-of-drawers, writing desk, and easy chair. The bathroom was spacious and well-fitted, with a fine glassed-in shower. Duke was pleased with the whole setup. After the massed living of the Army, the privacy of his own hotel room had been delightful to Duke in the beginning, but the sterile loneliness had started palling on him after several weeks of it. He was glad to have a congenial roommate again, and he found the clublike atmosphere of the place agreeable.

His first week was spent on double-dates with Garrick, routine commonplace engagements with Indiana school teachers and Maine nurses and New Hampshire office girls and the like. "The initiation period was the small-fry," Garrick explained. These evenings were smooth and uneventful and mildly pleasurable. The girls wanted to go to the Latin Quarter or the Diamond Horseshoe or the Copacabana perhaps, while others chose 21 or the Stork Club, and some elected to watch the antics in the Village Barn or the Lesbians in Tony Pastor's.

At the end of the week Duke Morey hadn't learned much except that the organization was conducted with streamlined efficiency, and thus far at least everything seemed to be honest and above-board. The young men lived in style and luxury, but the business was operated with strict military discipline, and

Garrick warned Duke against going AWOL at any time. Under the carefree easy-going surface of life in the brownstone building there was strict regimentation. The young cavaliers dreaded nothing more than being called in on the carpet before Ellinger and Kern and Zolnay.

In his second week Duke Morey became acquainted with the daytime work. Ellinger's switchboard was busy almost twenty-four hours a day, and escorts were assigned to morning and afternoon shifts, as well as night. The shift assignments were on a weekly basis, and each day they received instructions for the mission at hand.

Mornings usually meant sightseeing tours, museum and art galleries, zoos and aquariums and other points of interest. Unless you happened to draw a doll bent on curing a hangover via the-hair-of-the-dog method. Afternoons generally called for ball games, beaches, racetracks, amusement parks, or matinees, and with the sports-minded clients Duke derived most of his enjoyment. Imagine being well paid, he thought, to take a more or less beautiful girl out to watch the Yanks... This week also passed without any sign of underhanded activity, and Duke was becoming convinced that Ellinger's Escort Service was just what it proposed to be and nothing else.

On his own the third week, and back on the evening shift, Duke Morey began to encounter some of the odd female characters he had been hearing about. There was a highly neurotic widow from Detroit, young and attractive and completely sex-mad, and there was nothing dull about his session with her. Duke began to see what Clyde Vorse had meant about avoiding seduction, and to wonder how Ellinger's boys stood the pace.

She got Duke back to her hotel room, and said she'd go into the next room to make herself a drink. A minute later she called to Duke to come into the TV room. He walked in and there she was, with a drink, but also without a stitch of clothing. She wasn't bad looking, although she looked a little worse for her thirty or so years, but if she lacked a thing or two in build, she made it up in desire.

She just stood there, posing for Duke, sipping her drink. "C'mon, big boy," she said. "Let's see just *how* big you are." She sprang at Duke like a pantheress and started to undress him. He grabbed her hands and half pulled her to him. She thought he was being aggressive, but actually it was a defensive gesture by Duke. He knew what this woman was and what she stood for, and he had to figure a way out of making love to her without having her blow up, complain and lose him his job just when he figured he might be getting close to Ann.

She came at him again, and this time it was obvious what he was trying to do.

She drew back. "What are you doing?" she said. "You're being paid—and well—to escort me. That means doing whatever I want, wherever I want. What the hell is wrong with you anyway?"

Duke tried to pass it off. "It's my time of month, baby," he said.

She came at him, her breasts waggling, and slapped him on the face. "There!" she screamed. "You think you can make fun of me! There!" Her hand tore out scratching his shoulder deeply. Duke lost his temper. He grabbed her by the arm and snapped her back across the room. She didn't stop until she hit the wall. Then she just kind of slid down until she was sitting on the floor, dazed. "Oh, Christ," Duke muttered. "Now I've really screwed up." He looked at her as she came to her senses. He'd have to give her some of what she wanted or there'd be hell to pay with Ellinger. Duke went to her, picked her up, carried her to the bed. But he managed to satisfy her with only his deft hands.

The suburban housewife that Duke drew next was one Duke knew he couldn't even touch, though. She was hell-bent on avenging a night of faithlessness by her husband, and Duke wanted to send her home unravished. He wondered how many of the Ellinger boys would've passed up a pretty piece like that, especially with the way she acted after they left the club where they'd eaten dinner. They were walking and gradually she had led him to a deserted section. It was dark and she was pressing up against him as they walked. Duke tried to press back politely without arousing her or himself. His last bout, though, made it hard. The time before that with Jane made it even harder. The pickup afterward hadn't satisfied him.

All at once, the gal pulled him into an alley and threw her arms around him, pressing her lips to his. He decided nothing could come of it, so he went along. Suddenly she lifted her skirt high around her hips and moved back a few inches. "Do it to me—here—now?" she said. The flash of long tapering legs and nylons glimmering into garters and shapely panties was almost too much for Duke. "Take me!" she repeated. "Please—please take me here—now ..." She moved up against him. Duke pushed her away with an Herculean effort. "You don't want to do this," he said. "You don't want me." Somehow, he convinced her of it. It wasn't easy—for either of them.

Number Three for Duke was a crazy kid, on the lam from some ritzy private school to sample life in the raw, and she was plainly contemptuous of him and what Manhattan had to offer in the way of thrills and excitement. "You don't know from nothing here," she said. "You ought to go to a Dartmouth Winter Carnival or a Yale Prom and pick up a few pointers, boy."

"We used to have some pretty good house parties at Wisconsin," Duke Morey said mildly.

"Well, what happened to you since then?" the girl said. "You must've forgotten all you learned out there."

Duke knew he'd forgotten more than she'd learn in the next ten years—even with her provocative outlook—but the last thing he wanted to do was to play teacher to this immature kid. Duke got an inspiration, then. "I guess you think *sex* are the only thrills in life, sophomore," he said.

She looked at him, puzzled.

"Well," he said, "come with me. I'll show you what *real* excitement is."

Duke knew of a little opium den in the Chinese part of town where a guy handled supposedly poisonous snakes. He let them crawl all over him, even stuck their heads in his mouth. He proved they were poisonous by letting them bite a little mouse first and then the mouse died in a minute. Duke figured the mouse was already poisoned or doped with a slow acting killer, and that the snakes were as harmless as worms.

Sophomore liked the show, but still thought Duke could do better. "Look," she said. "Now let me show *you* some excitement. I'm staying with one of my aunts. She doesn't get along with my mother, so she doesn't tell my parents I'm here. Let's go back there." Duke protested mildly, but had to go along or look bad. When they got there, Auntie was sleeping in her room. Sophomore took Duke in the kitchen, turned on the radio, and turned off the lights. She took some liquor from a cabinet and poured them both a half glass of straight bourbon. She stood against the sink swallowing it, obviously trying to get drunk fast so that she could get up the courage to do what she wanted. As she stood there, Duke noticed for the first time how mammoth her breasts were. They'd be hanging at her hips when she was thirty, but right now they were erect and tantalizing, and amazingly big for such a short, rather slim girl. A minute later she drained her glass and put it down. "Come here," she purred. Duke walked to her, half hypnotized. "Let's dance, honey," she said, slurring her words a little. He put his arms around her waist and they started to sway to the music. "Put your hands on my breasts," she said. Duke would've done it anyway. He craved Jane, he needed and wanted Ann, but he was a man, all man, and he couldn't hold off every time—whether he wanted to or not. It was too much for him physically. Christ, he thought, what a job—of all jobs—for a man to have in order to find his sweetheart. He didn't think that too much longer, though, as his hands went up to Sophomore's tremendous bosom and began to knead the heaving womanhood that blossomed out from everywhere. She liked it, and arched her back against the sink, making her chest protrude all the more as Duke caressed it, worked it beneath his expert hands. "Bet you've never had those hands around a 32-D before, honey," she said, breathing a little heavier. Duke was the aggressor now. He didn't need any more coaxing. He unbuttoned her sweater, literally tore the bra off her. "That'll cost me $3.95, big boy," she purred in a feigned anger. Duke half grinned, but then his face dissolved into an eager tension as he bent her back even farther, holding both her arms behind her back with one of his giant hands, while the other roved over her heaving bosom. "Oh God, that's good," she whispered through little pearly teeth that were now grinding together. "That's real good." It was even better when Duke pulled her down to the kitchen floor and started to teach her things that never went on at any Dartmouth Carnival or Yale Prom. Just at the last possible moment, however a thought struck him. She was so eager—so wild over his advances. What if she were a virgin? What if this "experienced" act was just that—an act? He didn't want to be the one to take away this girl's virginity. She was no Jane—no Ann—that was for sure. She was headed the wrong way on a one way street, in fact, at high speed. But Duke didn't want to start her on her crash into traffic. "Give it to me, honey, give it to me!" she groaned into his ear. "I'm going to, honey," he said. "We're going to give it to each other. Now I'm really going to show you something."

"Wha—" Sophomore said, but Duke had already maneuvered into position. "Now, kid," he said, "do what I tell you to do when I tell you to do it. And leave the rest up to me."

"But—"

"Sophomore," he said, "I didn't bring any—you know—so it's got to be this way. Besides, this way I can keep an eye on your aunt's door." At the end, Ann and Jane revolved in front of his mind amidst a burst of stars. After it was over, Duke knew he'd have at least one repeat customer from the Ellinger service.

One was about all Duke would have, though. His next "escort" was a dizzy divorcee from the South who was beginning to gain weight and was getting a little desperate. She wanted to sleep with Duke, but more than that she wanted to marry him, producing a bankbook filled with astronomical figures to show him what he was missing by turning down her proposal. A few kisses, a few more compliments about her girlish figure and a promise to "consider" the proposal got Duke home safe here, even though the lady was rather peeved by evening's end.

The fifth female in this fantastic procession was a dark, lusty Latin lady of dubious mental balance, who drew a gun on Duke and threatened to shoot him when he turned down her advances. After living through Korea, Duke disliked the idea of being shot in this senseless fashion, and explained desperately that a war wound had left him impotent. "What the hell you doin' in this racket, then?" asked the lady. "Beat it, you big fake, before I give you a *real* wound!"

Number Six was a dipsomaniac, a fugitive from Alcoholics Anonymous, who passed out just as she was presenting Duke with a sexual problem. She slumped over with one of his hands tucked inside her bra.

Seven—and last, for the time being, anyway—was a half mad artist. She kept wanting Duke to strip and pose in the nude, so she could paint his "soul." When he laughed it off, she got mad and tried to kick him in his "soul." He deftly ducked and called a cab, a bit disgusted with the whole thing.

CHAPTER SIX

"What the hell's the matter with women anyway?" Duke asked his roommate. "Are they all nuts?"

"Most of 'em, one way or another," grinned Tom Garrick.

"How can you respect any of them, after working in this business?"

"Who wants to respect 'em?" Garrick said, laughing. "The trouble with American men is they've always respected women more than they deserve. Don't let it get you down, Duke. It's all in a lifetime."

"Well, I can see that Ellinger Escorts really earn their money," Duke Morey said, with conviction.

"That's right, Duke," agreed Tom Garrick. "There's no such thing as easy money in this merry madhouse of a world."

"Maybe the atom bomb is making women worse," Duke muttered.

"I doubt it," said Garrick. "They've always been bad enough, but we've always tried to put them on a pedestal."

"I'm not going to last long in this league, I know that."

"Buck up, boy, your'e doing fine."

"Don't kid me, Tom," said Duke wearily. "This isn't for me, and that's for sure."

"You just ran into a rough week, Duke. You'll draw some nice sane girls yet, who'll renew your faith and hope in women."

"I doubt it, Tom. When you get seven out of seven screwballs, your luck's really run out."

"Don't take it so big and serious, Duke," said Tom Garrick. "Laugh it off and forget it—like I do. I used to have all the finer sensibilities myself, but they got blunted and dulled."

Duke Morey shook his crewcut head. "I'll never like it, Tom."

"But think of all the money you can save in a year or so. You couldn't do it in any other kind of business, Duke."

They were talking and smoking in their room, Garrick stretched on his bed in silk pajamas and robe, Duke Morey slouched in an easy chair in slacks and T-shirt. It was cosy and homelike in the mellow lamplight, with books and magazines and their possessions scattered about. They got along well and had grown close and friendly. Despite his dissatisfaction with the work and his thwarted yearning for both Ann and Jane, Duke felt a sense of contentment as he lounged there puffing on his favorite pipe.

Making discreet inquiries, Duke Morey had tried to find some member of the organization who remembered Ann Norvill, but to date he had been unsuccessful. There were at least a hundred escorts in the place, he estimated, and that complicated his efforts.

Checking with the Bureau of Missing Persons, Duke learned there was no report on Ann. A half-dozen other young women had turned up missing in the past two weeks, and Duke listed their names with the intention of keeping his eyes and ears open around Ellinger's brownstone building.

"They don't seem to make the papers," he had remarked.

"I guess they aren't news," the clerk had replied, indifferently.

So, Duke thought biterly, if their names aren't news, they can vanish right and left, and to hell with them. Very convenient for a ring of white-slavers…He knew it wasn't that bad, of course. Men actually worked around the clock to trace missing individuals, especially if there were interested people behind them. But strange girls could disappear in New York, without anyone seeming to notice or care, until belated appeals came in from hometown and families hundreds of miles away. To involve matters even more, many of the people, particularly the wealthy and prominent ones, wished to avoid newspaper publicity at any cost. All this made it easier for a kidnapping and blackmailing syndicate.

Duke Morey discovered that he missed Jane Tolman, as well as Ann, and wished she'd phone the agency and request a date with him, although they had decided it would be best to wait until he'd been there a month anyway. He wondered if Lolly Durand was still playing around with Borchek and Castelli. If so, they had probably converted her into a drug addict by now, and had her well on her way toward a life of prostitution. Well, he had enough troubles without worrying over that foolish blonde...

Someone rapped on the door then, and Duke Morey was surprised to see Gene Desmond and Park Lomax enter on his invitation. They occupied the position of field officers in this service, liaison between the top brass and the rank-and-file, and there was something about them that Duke didn't like or trust. They wore sport shirts, slacks and loafers, and both had a casual elegance in any kind of clothing. Duke moved from the chair to his bed, leaving them the easy chairs. Lomax lounged lazily in one of them, but Desmond remained standing.

"What have you got against women, Morey?" asked Desmond.

"What do you mean?" Duke encountered, in surprise.

"We've had some complaints on you this past week."

Duke Morey laughed softly. "Dissatisfied clients?"

"It's not funny, Morey," said Desmond sternly. "This agency is not a joke. Mr. Ellinger wanted me to speak to you. What's the matter, that you can't seem to get along with our patrons?"

"I thought I got along pretty well, considering the fact that they were all whacky."

"You might consider some of our best customers whacky, but they're still good business and we can't afford to lose them." Gene Desmond paced to and fro, handsome features set and blue eyes icy, a magnificent figure of young manhood. He didn't smoke or drink, but was reputed to be absolutely ruthless and insatiable with women. He had no interest in sports, except for the physical culture exercises that kept him fit and strong. Desmond had little interest in anything besides himself and the opposite sex. It would be, Duke concluded, very easy to hate this big arrogant strikingly handsome fellow.

"You want my resignation, Desmond?" he asked, quiet but taut.

"No, I simply want to get to the bottom of this, Morey, and find out why you aren't clicking right."

"Maybe I'm not cut out to be a gigolo."

"Why did you apply for a job then? You knew what kind of work it was. You knew what you were getting into. Perhaps you had some ulterior motive for joining us, Morey?"

"No, I just needed a job."

Tom Garrick straightened up on the edge of his bed. "Look, Gene. Duke had a run of screwloose dames last week. They'd have given anybody trouble. He'll be all right when he hits some sane clients."

Gene Desmond frowned at him. "I wasn't asking you, Garrick."

Tom Garrick's fine grave face hardened. "This isn't the gestapo, is it, Desmond? I've still got a right to speak, haven't I?"

"Take it easy, Tom," drawled Park Lomax, lifting his pale sleepy eyes and blond head, as he spoke for the first time. He was mild and reticent, lazy and languid acting, yet Duke felt again that there was a streak of wildness and toughness behind Lomax's mild manner.

Gene Desmond's cold superior stare flicked from Garrick to Morey. "Are you normal sexually, Morey?" he inquired flatly.

Duke Morey rose from the bed with a thin smile. "Are you inferring that I'm not?" he demanded, suddenly eager to lash out and smash that haughty carved face and lofty dark head.

"I'm not inferring anything, I'm asking." Desmond gestured, with weary patience. "There must be something that makes you so invulnerable to feminine charms, Morey. You turned most of the broads down."

"Am I supposed to jump into bed with every coked-up, drunked-up female maniac I go out with?" Duke asked, gray eyes ablaze. "If I am, you can shove this job and the whole filthy business, Desmond!"

Desmond gestured again. "That's not the point, Morey. Not all of our customers want a man to go to bed with them. But *when* they do—and they're young and attractive and well-stacked—is that too much of a hardship for you to endure?"

"I was resigned to being a gigolo—for a while," Duke said. "But I'll be goddamned if I'll be a male whore!"

"You don't have to be, Morey," protested Desmond. "But once in a while you could throw a lay into them, I should think. I don't understand you at all, Morey. Your attitude's all wrong, I'm afraid."

"Fire me then."

"Please, Morey. Can't we discuss this in a calm civilized fashion?"

Duke Morey sighed, and sank back onto the bed. "Maybe I'm in love, Desmond. Did you ever think of that?"

"So what?" Gene Desmond said, laughing without sound or mirth. "A little piece on the side now and then won't hurt you or your girl either. It might help to preserve her chastity, and bring her unsullied to the altar."

"Very funny," Duke said. "Get to the point, if any, Desmond. I'm sick of this kind of talk."

Desmond eyed him with menace. "I hope I'm not going to have trouble with you, fellah."

Duke Morey stood up again. "Any time you want to start some, I'm ready, boy."

From the leather chair, Park Lomax waved a limp slender hand. "Don't be so tough all the time, Duke," he drawled softly. "Makes me nervous, all this tough stuff."

"Give him a chance then, you guys," put in Tom Garrick. "He's only been soloing a week. What do you expect, an ace in that time?"

"All right, all right," Gene Desmond said, flashing his professional smile of insincere warmth and charm. "We're getting nowhere here, Park, we might as well call it a night. But we'll be watching you, Morey—and hoping for improvement."

Duke Morey grinned, with faint mockery. "Don't expect too much. When I lay somebody, it'll be somebody I really want. Not just any oversexed slut that's paying for it."

"You'll change your mind and your attitude," Desmond said, with cool assurance. "You'll change, Morey, or you won't last here."

"That worries me," Duke said.

"Bear one thing in mind, fellah," advised Gene Desmond. "Once you're in here, it's not so easy to get out as you might think."

"Like the Foreign Legion," suggested Duke Morey.

Park Lomax rose with lithe grace, and smiled pleasantly at him. "You're a smart boy, soldier. But smart boys are a dime a dozen around here. Happy dreams, boys." He moved to the door with catlike ease.

Gene Desmond smiled like a politician and said, "No hard feelings, Morey. We're all in this together," and strode majestically out after Lomax. Watching the closed door, Duke found his fists were clenched tight and white-knuckled, his forearm muscles ridged to the elbow, with a compulsion to spit from his dry mouth and throat.

"You could have soft-pedaled some of that stuff, Duke," said Tom Garrick, carefully lighting another cigarette.

"Why?" murmured Duke Morey, polishing the bowl of his pipe. "I'm not going to take anything from Desmond. The way I see it, Lomax is the rough one in that pair."

"Yeah, Lomax is rough all right," Tom Garrick said, brooding over some secret knowledge of his own. "Desmond's a big blowhard, but he's a bad one, too ..."

It was soon after that when Duke Morey received his first call from Stella Leeds, a rather tall and strangely fascinating girl, with coppery red hair and jade green eyes, slim and willowy yet strong and superbly curved, cool and poised and thoroughly sophisticated. The most attractive one so far, and the most puzzling. It was impossible to place Stella Leeds in any specific category. She was too deep and complex for that.

Duke was really interested this time. He would have been less than human, if he hadn't been, regardless of Ann Norvill and Jane Tolman. For Stella Leeds was like a composite of all lovely sirens, and every man who came in contact with her was instantly aware of her alluring charms ... Afterward, Duke Morey could see how it was all planned and arranged, but at the time all he could see was her unusual and intriguing features framed in the auburn hair, and the flawless lines and infinite grace of her seductive body.

CHAPTER SEVEN

His first repeat call came from Stella Leeds, and Tom Garrick congratulated him, while Desmond and Lomax, Vorse and Frappier, seemed to regard him with more respect. Duke Morey found he was anxious to see Stella again and it troubled him, made him feel guilty toward Ann Norvill, and in a lesser degree toward Jane Tolman. But he could not help it. Stella Leeds had something for him, something too powerful and consuming to be resisted. Desire had sprung alive between them the first moment they were together, and it was more than just physical, too. Duke liked simply being with her and talking with her. There were responsive chords in their minds, as well as their bodies.

Stella talked well on almost any subject. Like Duke, she read a great deal, and from a variety of diversified books and periodicals. Also she liked all sports and knew baseball, football and basketball, even better than Jane Tolman and Ann Norvill did, and was herself an accomplished golfer, tennis player and swimmer. Thus they had much in common and their hours together were never dull, but somehow Duke Morey was half-afraid of her at odd intervals. Stella Leeds was almost too calm and controlled, too poised and self-assured and perfectly at ease, in all circumstances.

"What are you doing in this business, Duke?" she asked, as they danced in a roof-garden ballroom high over the city.

"Earning a living."

"I can't figure you in this line. You don't belong, Duke. You're different than the others."

"You know the others?" he asked. "You make a practice of this, Stella?"

She laughed, a cool rippling sound. "I know a few of them. A girl gets tired of her own crowd and wants an occasional change ... Don't you approve—of this?"

"Sure, it's all right—I guess."

"See what I mean about you?" Stella Leeds said, smiling up at him. "You neither like nor approve of this. You're really an old-fashioned, clean-cut, outdoor American boy. This isn't your field, Duke. You know it, and you hate it ... What are you doing it for?"

Duke Morey shrugged slightly. "Money, I suppose. I had to do something. Wasn't quite good enough for professional baseball. Never did go for hard work."

"It's more than that, Duke," she persisted.

For an instant he was tempted to tell her the truth about Ann Norvill's disappearance and his search for her, but then something cautioned him against it. Stella knew some of his fellow-escorts, and she might spill it to them. It was better not to reveal it to anyone.

They left the polished floor and wandered outside, to lean on a stone balustrade and stare out over the myriad sparkling lights of Manhattan, the vast towers honeycombed golden in the night, the streets blazing canyons far below. Overhead the bright tilted crescent moon and the glittering stars had the unreal look of a stage setting. The music floated out sadly on the dark balmy breeze.

"I like you, Duke," said Stella, frankly and earnestly. "This isn't a line, and I don't expect anything from you. I just happen to like you ... Will you believe that I'm your friend?"

"Why yes, sure, Stella," he said uncertainly. "Of course, I will. I—I like you, too."

"Never mind that, Duke." She gestured sparsely. "You've got a girl somewhere, I can tell. But that doesn't matter. Why don't you get out of this racket, Duke? Before it's too late."

"But why? What do you mean? There isn't anything really *wrong*, is there?"

"No, maybe not," Stella Leeds said. "But it'll do something to you, Duke. Change you, harden you, make you like the rest of them. That shouldn't happen to you. I don't want it to happen. You mustn't let it happen, Duke!" Her tone was low, deep and urgent.

"Well, I never intended to stay in this very long," he said, in all honesty. "I'll get out as soon as I have some money, Stella."

"Make it soon, Duke. Don't hang around too long. Don't let it get you."

"I won't," Duke Morey promised. "Don't worry about me, Stella."

"You've seen the others. You know what I mean, Duke." She shuddered, ever so slightly. "That little slimy reptile of a Frappier, and the cold cruel vulture of a Vorse. And Gene Diamond's like a big beast, they say, and Park Lomax is dead inside—and deadly all through. And the sly slick lecherous Rudy Valance."

"Tom Garrick's all right, Stella," said Duke.

"Yes, I guess he is, one of the better ones. But he's been there too long, Duke. It's getting him, just as it's getting Bill Howell and Sid Pawley and all the rest."

"You ever see the big shots? Ellinger and Kern and Zolnay?"

Stella inclined her coppery head, shimmering red-gold in the lights from the ballroom. "Yes, I've seen them. You look at them, Duke. Their faces will tell you what kind of a business it is. A child could read the greed and evil in their faces."

"Well, it's only for a little while, Stella."

"There are others that you don't see," Stella Leeds went on. "The bodyguards and gunmen, the strong-arm boys and killers...Be careful, Duke. They're always suspicious of new men there."

"You seem to know a lot about Ellinger's, Stella," he said wonderingly.

She smiled. "I've been around here most of my life, Duke." She began to sing, in a soft throaty voice: *"East Side, West Side, all around the town…"* Breaking off abruptly, Stella Leeds said. "I'm tired, Duke, and I know your leg must be tired. Let's go to my place and relax over a few quiet drinks."

"Sounds mighty good to me, gal," said Duke Morey, with a boyish grin.

Her apartment was smart, sumptuous and richly appointed, like nothing Duke had ever seen outside of the movies, yet Stella made him feel instantly comfortable and at home there, while she went to the small bar and made a couple of highballs. The furniture was easy and relaxing, as well as fashionable. There was a fireplace, a book-lined wall, a Capehart combination, and a few paintings by Inness, Winslow Homer, John Sloan, George Bellows, and Luigi Lucioni…Duke approved her art, as well as her literature, which included Hemingway, Faulkner, Dos Passos, Kantor, Steinbeck, Fitzgerald, Wolfe, Wilder, Marquand, and Longstreet, among many others of his favorites.

The drinks were smooth but strong, the chairs restful and comforting, the lights soft and soothing, and the soundproof walls afforded real privacy and solitude. Duke Morey lay back in utter relaxation and quiet pleasure, disturbed only by the heady tenuous thread of Stella's perfume and the deep excitement of her nearness. There was a hunger in him that he tried to still and subdue, but it wouldn't stay down.

They talked of many things in the fragrant golden dimness, as the bonded bourbon warmed their blood, stirred and sharpened their minds, colored their thoughts and loosened their tongues. Of families and childhood and schooldays, friends and places far and near, memories from the past and dreams of the future, life and love and death. They were warm and happy together, wistful and sad together, and always drawn nearer, dearer and closer.

Duke studied her face over the rim of his glass, until each lovely detail was etched in his brain. The coppery hair curling back from the broad pure brow, and the slight exotic slant of the green eyes, that crinkled and tilted even more when she smiled. The proud straight nose, the flare of the high cheekbones, the shadowy hollowed cheeks, and the firm clean line of the jaw and chin and throat. The exquisite curving sweep of the wide lush mouth ... And her body, slim and supple with full high-thrusting breasts and strong hips, the flowing curves from shoulders to ankles, the long graceful silken legs.

Then they had abandoned their chairs to lounge side by side on the divan, tingling with the electric touch of their shoulders and thighs, enwrapped in a kind of singing flame. Duke Morey was never quite sure how it started. They must have drunk more than they realized, although they were quite sober ... Somehow, all of a sudden they were in one another's arms, mouths and bodies ground together, as if in a desperate despairing attempt to merge into one, and everything else was burned away into obscurity. Nothing left but their need of each other, which could not be denied.

After a lost timeless interlude of mingled delight and anguish, Duke realized Stella Leeds was struggling to free herself. He let her go, thinking it would end this way and he'd remain faithful to Ann Norvill—and in a way, to Jane Tolman—in spite of himself. But Stella was whispering breathlessly: "Not here ... not this way. You wait a minute, darling. Then come, come to me." She rose with quick lissome ease and went into the bedroom, and Duke Morey got up in a daze to pace the floor, sheathed in heat, burning with desire. If Stella had taken a little longer, his heart might have slowed and his blood ceased racing like liquidfire, and sanity might have returned to him. But her voice was already calling him, "Duke! All right, darling," and to save his life he couldn't have held back from answering that soft urgent call.

Duke walked into the bedroom, ripping off his tie and fumbling with shirt buttons. Stella Leeds was lying naked on the opened bed, glowing golden and lovely against the white sheet, her hair flaming. Her legs were spread wide apart, and Duke noticed the nipples on both her breasts were already hard and erect. Both hands were on her hips. An amber lamp shown softly from the night-table by the head of the bed. Duke reached for the light, but Stella said:

"No, Duke. Leave it on. I want to see you, darling."

"Yes," he said thickly, stripping off the rest of his clothes. "I want to see you too, Stella."

Then he was on the bed with her and once more they were crushed and locked together, their mouths fused and their bodies blending. And then her hands were not on her own hips, but on his, urging them on and on. This time there was no clothing between them, and every external thing was obliterated by the shattering soaring wonder of their union...

Afterward, a long time afterward, drained and exhausted in the damp sheets, they drifted into a sleep as deep and dreamless and peaceful as death itself.

It was noontime the next day, when Duke Morey got back to Ellinger's Escort Service. In the lobby Gene Desmond and Park Lomax, the latter smoking an after-lunch cigar, met him with wise knowing smirks, and Desmond said, in a friendly way: "I guess you made the grade all right, Morey. You're really one of us now, fellah."

Wondering about this remark and smarting with resentment, Duke went on into the dining room and joined Tom Garrick at their usual table. Garrick looked up, with a wide grin. "Well, Stella must have given you the full treatment, son. It's something to remember, isn't it? One for the book, Duke."

"What the hell is this?" asked Duke Morey, hoarse with anger. "Does everybody in town know Stella Leeds?"

"Everybody in Ellinger's, at least," Garrick said. "But what do you care, Duke? You had one of the best lays in New York. Didn't you enjoy it?"

"How come all these drips know her, Tom?"

"Could be they've all laid her. Matter of fact, I think they have."

"I don't believe it," Duke Morey said.

"Listen, Duke. Why would I lie about that?"

"You've had her yourself, then?"

"Sure, I have," Tom Garrick said. "It's no secret around here."

"I still can't believe it," Duke insisted stubbornly, knowing it must be true but refusing to admit it.

Garrick smiled, his rather gaunt grave cheeks creasing to his amber eyes. "Did she leave the light on, Duke? Didn't she want to see you? Stella likes it a lot better with the light on."

"I'll be goddamned," Duke Morey said mildly, shaking his tawny closecut head. "A girl like that. A smart girl like Stella Leeds. How can she be such a tramp, Tom?"

Garrick laughed gently. "Who knows, Duke? You must've seen cases like her before. Too much money, too many hormones, too much Freud."

"Yeah, but I never understood 'em."

"Nobody understands 'em. But they happen, they exist. And I suppose, they're to be pitied, Duke."

"I suppose so," Duke Morey said wearily, feeling sick to his stomach. "Well, live and learn. I thought I was really getting something."

"You were, Duke, you did," declared Tom Garrick. "They don't come much better than Stella in that line."

"It's nothing I want, if all these jerks have had it. Even Frappier and Valance, probably? Desmond and Lomax, too?"

"Yes, they've all been there, Duke," said Garrick. "Desmond was one of the first. Frappier tells quite a story about his experiences there. Claims Stella's quite unorthodox, at times."

"Excuse me, Tom." Duke Morey stood up and turned away, really sick in the pit of his stomach now.

"Aren't you going to have any lunch, Duke?"

"No, I don't feel like eating." Duke strode away and climbed the stairs to his room.

In the bathroom he felt like vomiting, and gagged and retched but nothing came up. He went out and threw himself across his bed, and waited for the nausea to go away. *Goddamn her,* he thought bitterly. *Damn all of the dirty slutting no-good bitches to hell*...Duke Morey wanted more than ever to find Ann Norvill now, and in her absence he had a need and longing for little Jane Tolman. Somebody clean and decent; honest and true.

CHAPTER EIGHT

It was a relief and a pleasure to find Jane Tolman's name and address on his assignment card one morning, calling for a double tour of duty, afternoon and evening. Duke Morey requisitioned and got one of the company cars, and drove down to Jane's apartment in Greenwich Village. They were delighted to see one another again, but Duke managed to keep their embrace casual and friendly.

"I had an awful time getting you, Duke," said Jane Tolman. "You must be getting very popular with the paying clientele."

"Have to call early to catch me," Duke Morey grinned. "The demand for my services is growing enormous. But seriously, Janie, I'm so sick and tired of women, it's hard for me to properly appreciate being with you."

"Quit kidding, mister," laughed Jane. "You're probably having the time of your life. But have you run across anything at all on Ann?"

"Not a thing," he admitted gloomily. "Nobody there seems to know a thing about Ann Norvill, and I can't get at the files. It looks like a blank wall, Jane."

"Well, Lolly Durand's gone now," Jane said miserably. "She went out two nights ago and never came back. Disappeared like Ann did."

"Was she out with those same two gorillas?"

"I suppose so. She promised not to see them any more, but she'd been with them a lot."

"Hitting the dope?"

"I don't know how bad, Duke. I smelled marihauna on her several times."

"It was bound to happen, in her case," Duke Morey said. "She was practically begging for it, Janie, running around with her neck hanking out a mile."

"But where do you think she is?" asked Jane Tolman. "What could they have done with her, Duke?"

"It's hard to tell, Jane," he said. "The first step used to be Troy. I've seen them fifteen and sixteen years old, in houses up there, real pretty kids, too. But Dewey closed Troy up during World War Two. They might ship her to Albany though, he didn't clean that town up much. Or she might land in Detroit, Toledo, Chicago, and points west. Or south in Washington or Baltimore."

"You aren't very encouraging," protested Jane.

"What's the use? If you got her back, she'd go right out and do it all over again. That's her destiny, Jane. I told you where that blonde would end up."

"You've grown bitter, Duke."

"Bitter!" Duke Morey laughed, without merriment. "The more women I see, the more I respect dogs. And the more sorry I feel for the poor guys that have to marry them."

"You don't see a representative element," Jane said.

"We see a lot of them though. An awful lot of them, from all over America. It's not a pretty picture, Janie."

"It's not a pretty world, Duke. Let's go dancing."

On Jane Tolman's insistence, they had dinner at home in her apartment, and it tasted better than all the extravagant ten dollar meals that Duke Morey had been eating of late. In the evening some impulse sent them to the Village Barn, possibly in an effort to take Jane's mind off the unfortunate Lolly Durand, and there they drank slowly and watched the square dances and the crazy clowning in which inebriated members of the audience took part.

The highlight was the hobby-horse race for women, and as they lined up astride the wooden mounts Duke Morey was startled and disgusted to see Stella Leeds, very drunk, laughing hilariously and straddling one of the little horses, her magnificent legs exposed halfway up the thigh. The mounts were designed to furnish leg-shows for the customers, of course, and the riders were all in various stages of intoxication and heedless of exposure, some of their skirts hiked up high enough to reveal the color of their silk panties.

"Women!" muttered Duke Morey. "Exhibitionists all."

"That red-headed one looks familiar," Jane Tolman mused. "And she's been eyeing you ever since we got here, Duke. What gives there?"

"Yeah, she hired me one night, that's all," Duke said acidly.

"Fine leg she's showing there," Jane remarked dryly.

"She's got all the equipment, super de luxe. And not a shred of decency of common sense or self respect."

"My, you *are* bitter, Duke!"

"It's a bitter world," Duke Morey said, with a somber smile. "Especially from Ellinger's Escort Service."

The race started, the women bouncing and rocking wildly in the tiny saddles, their shrill cries rising and their skirts flouncing ever higher, while the spectators cheered and roared with laughter at the ridiculous spectacle. Wooden horses toppled and girls rolled on the waxed floor, legs in the air or widely sprawling, dresses bunched around their waists and sheer silken shorts bared to the bright lights. Stella was leading the field when her mount went over and she fell headlong, sliding on the slippery surface, skirt awry above her full buttocks and splendid thighs. The crowd howled louder than ever at this display, and Duke said, "Women!" again, swearing under his breath, his cheeks inflamed under the tan and his ears rimmed with fire.

At last the race was over, with only two riders finishing, and the drunken winner jumped out of the saddle and did a few grinds and bumps, her dress flaunted high around her hips, and the audience hooted, whistled and jeered, and resumed drinking at their tables around the floor.

"God," murmured Duke Morey. "You see what I mean about women, Jane?"

"Yes, I see, Duke," she said quietly, and excused herself to go to the ladies' room.

"Be sick for me while you're in there," Duke said, and slumped back in his chair, staring at the glass in his long brown fingers, moving it idly in a diamond design on the tabletop. Home to first and second and third and home plate again. *If I'd only had enough stuff to be a big league ball player,* he thought ruefully.

A shadow fell across the table, and a familiar perfume stung his nostrils. Duke Morey looked up and saw Stella Leeds standing there, and his heart hammered and his throat constricted. "That was a very pretty performance," he said, nodding his sandy head and narrowing his gray eyes. "Very edifying indeed, Stella."

She slipped into the chair beside him. "I did it all for you, Duke. When I saw you come in, I decided to ride."

"Thanks a lot. I really appreciate that. I was proud I knew you."

"You know all about me now, don't you?"

"Not all, probably, but enough."

"I knew you would, Duke," she sighed. "As soon as you stayed with me. If I'd sent you home, you wouldn't have heard a thing about me at Ellinger's. But I couldn't help it, Duke, I couldn't..."

"Sure, I know. I swept you right off your feet, baby. My first conquest, under the Ellinger banner."

"Don't, Duke, please don't," Stella Leeds said. "I—I could still be your friend, if nothing more."

"Why not?"

"And I still say, get out of Ellinger's."

"You ought to know, kid," Duke Morey said. "You've been through the whole force. Even the slimy little Frappier, they say. Not to mention that big beast of a Desmond."

Stella Leeds tossed her coppery red head. "What did you expect, a virgin?"

"Never! Neither that nor the other extreme—which I got. You'd better go, Stella."

"I'm not good enough to meet your girl, Duke?"

"She's not my girl. Just a friend."

"She'd like to be your girl, if she isn't," Stella said. "She looks very nice and sweet, Duke."

"She is," Duke Morey said. "She admired you, too. Your horseback riding and your legs especially."

Stella's scarlet lips thinned. "Go to hell, you smug bastard!"

"If there's any two things I'm not, it's what you just called me. Good night, babe. Better luck with your next horse. Even Arcaro loses once in awhile."

"You're so funny, I could die laughing."

"So long, Stella."

Stella Leeds flung back the chair and stood up. "The time's coming when you're going to need help—and from me. Well, I'll be there, Duke. And I won't even hold this against you. Because I still like you, and I still want to be your friend."

"Thanks, Stella. I appreciate that even more than I did your riding for me." Duke Morey rose, as Jane Tolman returned to the table, and introduced the two girls.

There was an awkward moment, and then Stella laughed and said: "Duke's been telling me off for disgracing myself in that silly race. Well, I must be going. It was nice meeting you."

"Why, I thought you did real well," Jane Tolman said soberly. "You got the biggest hand of all when you took that dive."

Stella Leeds' green eyes flashed ominously. "You, too?" she said, her lips curling on the brilliant white teeth. "Well to hell with both of you!" She strode off with fluid grace, and Jane glanced after her with genuine admiration.

"She's really something, Duke! I don't blame you a bit."

"Blame me for what?"

"I guess you know, Duke. A man would be a fool to pass up anything like that."

"Damnation to all females," Duke Morey said, with quiet intensity. "Even you, Janie, even yourself."

They were finishing their drinks in thoughtful silence, when Jane Tolman suddenly cried: "Duke! I remember now where I saw your red-headed friend! She was coming out of Ellinger's. I was in the Rendezvous one afternoon, watching that brownstone building. It was after Ann disappeared. The redhead came out with three men and got into a big car and rode away."

"Are you positive, Janie?"

"Yes, I am. I knew I'd seen her somewhere, and that was it, Duke."

"What did the men look like?"

"One was fattish and bloated looking with horn-rimmed glasses. I took particular notice because I was looking for Ann, and I knew she'd been dating someone from that Escort Service. One was short and broad with a big hooked nose. The other was tall and skinny with reddish hair, I think."

"You've got 'em tagged, Janie," said Duke Morey. "Ellinger and Zolnay and Kern. So she is tied up with them some way. And she was trying to pump me about why I joined the agency. Stella Leeds could probably tell us right where Ann Norvill is—and how she got there." Duke's gray gaze swept the large smoky hall, but Stella was nowhere in sight… "Well, that may be the lead we're looking for, Janie. It's lucky we came here and saw Stella tonight. She must be working for Ellinger all right. Probably the go-between for him and the brothels. And I had her right in my hands once…"

"Your mind was on other things at the time, Duke," said Jane Tolman sweetly. "And I don't wonder at it a bit. With a build like that, she ought to be on the screen or the stage, or at least the burlesque boards. It isn't right to cover up a body like hers."

"Enough guys get to see it, don't worry," Duke Morey said dryly.

They were leaving the Village Barn when they bumped into Tony Castelli, alone and right in front of the place. Quicker than thought, Duke Morey's left hand flashed out and gripped the broad lapels of the hoodlum's coat, knotting them up tight under his throat. Before Castelli could recover from his surprise and regain his balance, Duke swung him around and thrust him backward, slamming him against the wall of the building with a jarring crash. The sidewalk was deserted except for them, the street empty of pedestrians with only a few cars swishing past.

Pinning Castelli there with his left hand, Duke Morey cocked his right fist and said: "Where's Lolly Durand? What did you and Borchek do with her?"

"How the hell—I know?" panted Castelli, writhing and straining to break loose, bringing his knee up suddenly toward Duke's groin.

Twisting away from that knee, Duke smashed his right fist into the man's dark scarred face, driving the greasy black head back into the wall. Again Duke slugged him and once more, with cold measured brutality. Blood gushed from Castelli's nose and mouth, as he sagged against the building.

"You're crazy," he gasped, drooling darkly. "You're nuts. I ain't seen Lolly. Don't know nothin' about her. Lemme go, you big bastard. I'll kill you for this."

"Where is she, Castelli? Where'd you put her, meatball? You know what the rap is for kidnapping? You could get life, Castelli. You could go to the chair."

"I ain't touched her, ain't seen her. Don't know nothin'—about her."

"You're a liar," Duke Morey said flatly, and struck that bleeding battered face again.

"Let him go, he won't talk, Duke," pleaded Jane Tolman. "Somebody's coming down the street now."

Tony Castelli heaved on the wall and thrashed out with his legs, kicking wildly at Duke's shins, and Duke gritted his teeth against the splintering pain, jamming the man back into the barrier and slashing right-handed at the evil mutilated features. As Duke drew his right back to finish him off, Jane cried out in warning and a heavy body surged into Duke's back, iron arms grappling his elbows and hauling him away from Castelli. Tony slid to his knees, scrambled up cursing and spitting blood, and faded quickly away into the shadows.

Duke Morey was still struggling to break that powerful hold, when the man on his back let go all at once. Whirling in red rage and about to swing at this unknown assailant, Duke saw big Gene Desmond towering there with Park Lomax smiling inscrutably at his shoulder. Dropping his hands, Duke said: "What's the idea, Desmond?"

"You ought to be more careful who you pick on, Morey," said Gene Desmond coldly. "That Wop's a bad one, a gunman. He'd just as soon kill you as spit on the sidewalk. What were you beating him up for anyway?"

"We had a little private trouble," Duke Morey said. "He had it coming to him. Don't ever jump me again, Desmond. I don't like that."

"For your own good, Duke," drawled Park Lomax. "That boy's a killer."

"That's right, Duke," said Gene Desmond. "And he's got a lot of friends who are killers, too. If they'd come along, you'd be dead on this sidewalk. And the young lady might be there with you."

"All right, forget it," Duke Morey said, turning to the girl. "Sorry, Jane, I shouldn't have lost my temper like that. Miss Tolman, Mr. Desmond and Mr. Lomax."

"He was very insulting," Jane Tolman said, her voice shaking.

"I don't doubt it, Miss Tolman," said Desmond. "But he is a very dangerous character."

"Sometimes it's better to swallow insults than bullets," Park Lomax said, in his lazy drawl. "Torpedoes like him are bad, Miss."

"Well, I suppose I should thank you boys." Duke Morey said.

"Not at all, Morey," said Desmond. "We just don't want any of our fellahs getting blasted, that's all. Pleased to have met you, Miss Tolman. See you in the morning, Morey. We're looking for someone in the Barn here. Good night to you both."

They went inside, and Duke and Jane walked toward the company sedan that was parked nearby. "I can't figure that one," Duke Morey said. "They don't care that much about what happens to me. I've got an idea Desmond did it to help Castelli instead of me, Jane."

"I don't know, Duke. They seemed sincere and nice enough about it."

"Yeah, maybe they were," Duke said. "Castelli has got a rep, and Borchek or some of his other pals might have come along and given me the works. But it's funny, their showing like that, and just when I might've had Castelli ready to talk."

"He wasn't going to talk, Duke," said Jane Tolman.

"You can't ever tell, Janie," said Duke, rubbing his right-hand knuckles as they approached the car. "Tony's real proud of his teeth. He wouldn't want to lose them."

A voice rose behind them: "Just a minute, Morey," and they turned and watched Gene Desmond striding after them. "Sorry, but I wanted to add a word of warning," he said, halting close to Duke. "Don't ever jump a gorilla like that unless you've got a gun, Morey. You don't carry one, do you?" With pretended playfulness, Desmond frisked him with professional speed and care, laughing as he did so.

"No, I don't," Duke Morey, reaching swiftly under Desmond's left arm. "But maybe I will hereafter." Desmond recoiled, hands jerking up.

Gene Desmond tried to mask his anger. "In this neighborhood, it's not a bad idea. Good night again, folks." He wheeled and stalked back to the entrance of the Village Barn.

"You see, Janie, something's going on under the surface. They wanted to make sure I wasn't packing a gun," Duke unlocked the car door.

"Well, you weren't, Duke. So it doesn't matter."

"But Desmond was, Janie," said Duke, helping her in and going around to climb in behind the wheel. "He had a rod on him. And he didn't like it much when I frisked him back and felt it."

"I don't know, Duke. I don't like it," Jane said. "I'm afraid of what you're getting mixed up in."

He grinned and started the motor. "I can take care of myself all right, baby."

"Yes, I guess you can," Jane Tolman said. "I never knew you could be so hard and brutal, Duke."

"How else can you fight people like that, Janie?" asked Duke Morey.

When they got back to Jane's apartment later, Duke knew he should leave before anything started, but after his sordid experiences with the oddballs he'd been forced to play gigolo to, he badly needed a real woman. He stood inside the door with her for a moment, holding her around the waist, their lips pressed together, swaying with her in time to the breeze coming in through the darkness around the livingroom window. Jane wanted Duke more in that moment than she ever had before, but she still couldn't make the first move. Maybe she had been too aggressive already, she thought to herself. But as Duke's arms hardened about her, she felt her hips swaying up and back ever so slightly in a movement all their own unconnected with the swaying of her body and Duke's. She knew she must stop then and there or else—

Duke felt it, felt the excitement of it pervade every inch of him, knew that he had to quit now or else spend the night with

Jane. He couldn't do that. He pulled away, abruptly. "I've got to run, Janie," he said.

"All right, Duke," she answered, trying to hide her feelings. "Be good." When the door closed, though, Jane knew that *good* was the last thing she would be. She breathed a sigh of relief that it had worked out this way, but she also clenched her fists as she felt the unbearable desire well up in her again.

She went into her room, felt a secret twinge of pleasure when she saw that Lolly wasn't home. She would be alone. For awhile, at least. She undressed, brushed her teeth, put up her hair, but it was all merely going through the motions. She knew that she couldn't escape the self-satisfaction of her own passion.

She decided to sleep naked. She got in the bed, lay there for a minute listening to the sounds outside. She threw off the covers. A breeze seemed to brush over her breast. She put her hand there, as if to protect it from that breeze. Then she pulled it away and pounded her fist into the sheets. "No, no, no!" she whispered. "I will not. I'll tie my hands if I have to!" She turned over on her stomach, moved restlessly against the bed. The sheet felt coarse but stimulating against her firm bosom. She became more rest-less. She pulled the pillow from the head of the bed and held it between her breasts and the sheet. But she couldn't help rubbing it against her body and in anger she thrust it down to the foot of the bed at her feet. It fell between her calves and she clenched it tight against them, rubbing the full length of her legs on it. She put her hands behind her head, not moving them, swearing to herself that she would not violate herself, that she would wait for Duke, or whatever man would someday be hers. But her legs smashed the pillow between them with a force that made hands unnecessary. It was three full hours later when she finally kicked the pillow casually to the floor and wondered, fleetingly, before falling off to a peaceful sleep, why Lolly hadn't come home yet.

CHAPTER NINE

Lolly Durand sprawled on her back on the disheveled bed, too shocked and exhausted to stir, staring at the ceiling with blank unseeing blue eyes. It seemed as if she had been staring at that same ceiling forever, but at least she was alone now. Her brain was fogged and reeling with drugs and liquor. Her body, naked under the soiled sheet, felt racked and bruised and beaten, ripped and torn up the middle. How long had she been here? How many times had she been violated, and by how many different men? She had lost all conception of time.

The body she had been so proud of no longer belonged to her. Flinging the sheet aside she looked down at her ravaged white flesh, the dark ugly bruises on the firm upstanding breasts, the soft rounded belly, the flaring hips and strong thighs. It was a dirty and shameful thing now. Lolly Durand would never feel clean again. All the water and perfumed soap and fragrant bath-salts in the world could not cleanse her. She moaned in utter misery and despair.

Why hadn't she listened to Jane Tolman and Duke Morey? Why had she persisted in flirting and playing, drinking and smoking reefers and smooching around with those two filthy rotten underworld characters? Now she was a total wreck, ruined beyond repair, her life ended at twenty-two.

Was that sex? she wondered dully. Was that the act I was so curious about and fascinated in and starved for? Is *that* what all talking and thinking and gossiping is done for, the love stories and dirty stories deal with, the great and beautiful romances culminate in? That horror, that panting, sweating, rutting, animal-struggle, that hot hideous plunging and heaving and striving, body to body, male against female. Could that be all there was to the eternal mystery and magic? What a joke, what a farce, what a mockery!...Men should pay for that, let it disrupt their lives and drive them to distraction, and women should give up homes and families and children for it. Why, it didn't make sense.

But it might be something, with the right man and the right woman, she supposed. Lolly Durand would never know about that now. It would always be ugly and horrible and evil, to her.

Again she could see those dark distorted faces over her, and feel the grinding weight, the savage ruthless ploughing of her innermost depths, and smell the odors of whiskey and sweat, armpit and crotch, while the bed leaped like a live thing, and the ceiling rose and fell and spun in crazy circles... *O God*, she thought, *Dear God, what have I done? How did I get here?...I can't stand this feeling. I can't live in this loathsome shell of flesh, that I hate and despise so. I'll have to kill myself. It's the only way out.*

Disjointed memories and visions came back to her, like something dimly remembered from a nightmare. At first there'd only been Tony Castelli and Franky Borchek, and she was too full of dope to recall much of it with any clarity. They took turns, one after the other, over and over again, on and on without cease. It must have lasted for hours. All night, all day?...She didn't know. Later, there were other men, other strained greedy faces and hairy muscular bodies, more like chimpanzees or apes than human beings, an endless merciless procession of them. And the others watching, smoking and drinking, laughing and jeering...*O God, I can't stand it. Please let me die.*

And their voices, sneering and contemptuous. "Get up, goddamn you! Get up and wash yourself. Gotta keep clean in this business...We're breakin' you in right, sister. You're goin' be a real pro, when we get done with you. We don't deliver no lousy amachoors ... You ain't got class enough to be a call girl. You're goin' in strictly on a piecework basis, Blondie. A five-buck whore in a five-buck whorehouse. Keep two, give the madam three. A good deal. Lay off the junk and you'll last a long time, baby, make a lotta money. Thirty-forty guys a day, a hundred and a half for the house, sixty-eighty bucks for *you*."

And more, and worse: "Thinka how much you're givin' away free here. Losin' money but gainin' experience. That's what counts, kid, the old experience. You ain't much good right now, but you'll learn. You got the body, but you don't know how to use it yet ... Get them legs up. Bring it up, babe, come up and meet it ... On your feet now, wash yourself good. Tired? At your age? What the hell you talkin' about? Wait'll you been puttin' out ten-fifteen years, baby. If the junk don't get you before that ... All right, back on the bed. Another customer comin' right up. Business is good, business is rushin'. Give the man a good ride, Lolly. Always give 'em a good time, they'll come back askin' for you. Sure, Lolly, you know that blonde with the big tits."

On and on, man after man, up to wash and back to bed, the smoky reeking room tilting and whirling dizzily about her, the pain stabbing deeper and deeper, blazing bright through the foul haze of drugs and alcohol, the stupor of exhaustion. *Why don't I die?* Lolly Durand had thought. *How much can a woman take anyway?* ... And, "Please, God, please let me die," Lolly Durand had prayed through clenched teeth.

But she was still alive, half-alive anyway, and Franky and Tony would be coming back soon with more drugs and liquor and men, and the terrible routine would start all over again, one after another, round after round.

Franky Borchek came back first, alone and smoking a big cigar, his arms full of packages and bags. "Christ, you look awful," he said. "Why didn't you get up and take a bath and fix yourself nice?"

"I couldn't," Lolly Durand whimpered. "I haven't got the strength."

He had some sandwiches for her but she couldn't eat anything solid, so he gave her a large double-brandy eggnog and Lolly drank that. It tasted cool and smooth, rich and good, even in a cardboard container.

"Franky, don't—don't do it to me any more," she pleaded. "Don't let them do it to me any more. I—I can't stand it, Franky. I'll die."

Borchek laughed aloud, throwing back his rough-cut blond head. "It takes a lot of that stuff to kill a broad. But I don't want no more of it, kid, you can count on that. I had all I want, sister. 'Specially the way you look now."

"Don't let them—don't let the others, Franky."

"They probably had enough, too. Unless that Tony wants some more. That Wop's the hungriest bastard for it I ever seen, Lolly. He can't get enough of it. He ain't hardly human."

"What—what you going to do with me—now?"

"We got a nice home for you, kid," Franky Borchek said. "Board and room and laundry. All you gotta do is what you been doin' right here for nothin', and you'll get two bucks a throw where you're goin'."

"I won't do it, Franky!" cried Lolly. "I won't stay in one of them houses."

"That's what they all say—at first. But they stay. They get so they like it. Where the hell else could you make fifty-sixty bucks a night?"

"What good's the money?" she sobbed.

Borchek laughed. "That's like askin' what good is fresh air to breathe and food to eat. You like fancy clothes and jewelry and perfume and stuff, don't you? You can buy all you want, and the best. You'll be settin' pretty, babe. You ain't never had it so good. And some of them whores even get married."

"Who'd marry—a girl like that?"

"Plenty of guys. Some suckers don't care, Lolly. They're gettin' a dame that knows all the tricks, and can do it every way there is. Which reminds me, you still got a helluva lot to learn."

"How can you learn, when they're coming at you like that?"

Franky Borchek grinned through the cigarsmoke. "It was kinda rugged, Lolly. But you didn't do bad. You took it pretty good ... Now I'll give you a little shot of junk. Fix you right up, make you feel fine, and you can take a bath and get dressed. Come on, you wanta look halfways decent, don't you?" He fumbled a heroin capsule out of a box.

Lolly Durand had bathed and dressed, and was looking almost fresh and pretty again, when the door opened and Tony Castelli stumbled in, his dark face gashed and swollen and crusted with blood, his shirt and tie and coat stained blackly with it. Franky Borchek lowered his whiskey glass and gaped at him.

"What the hell happened, Tony? You run into Sugar Ray Robinson?"

"That sonofabitch of a Morey!" mumbled Castelli. "I'm goin' to shoot the guts outa that guy one of these days."

"Where'd you see him?"

"Comin' outa the Village Barn. He muscled into me before I even saw him, and started workin' me over on the wall. Jane Tolman was with him. He had me by the neck and I couldn't do nothin'."

"Why didn't you kick him in the nuts, Tony" asked Borchek.

Castelli's sneer was grotesque. "Why didn't you? That night he knocked you ass over head down the stairs?"

"I'll get him yet," Borchek growled. "What happened then, Tony?"

"Desmond and Lomax come up, and Desmond grabbed Morey from behind and pulled him off me, and I powdered outa there."

"Is it all set to deliver this piece of goods?"

"I didn't wait to find out for sure, but we're goin' to deliver her," Tony Castelli said. "Soon as I get cleaned up a little here. I'm sick of seein' her around."

Lolly Durand smiled at him, her blue eyes unnaturally large and bright. "Don't you want to go to bed, Tony?" she asked, mockingly.

"Not with you," Castelli said. "Not ever again with you, baby. I've had it. Way up to here."

Borchek laughed and poured two more drinks. "Don't tell me you got sick of it, Tony. I never thought I'd see that time come."

"All I can think of is that Duke Morey," muttered Castelli. "I hate him so much it makes me sick in the belly. I ain't goin' to feel right again until I see him in the ditch with his guts full of lead, Franky."

"That's just where that boy's goin' to wind up, Tony," said Borchek. "And here's to it, chum. Wash your face and change your shirt now, and we'll get goin'. I'll feel a lot better when this bitch is off our hands for good."

Lolly Durand, the dope and brandy working in her, was feeling high and gay and reckless. "You boys'll come to see me, won't you? After I start working?"

"For five bucks?" Tony Castelli spat on the floor. "I wouldn't give you five cents for all night. If you don't get better awful fast, they'll heave you right outa that two-bit whorehouse. It ain't enough to have a good build and a big pair of tits, baby."

Lolly lifted her bright golden head. "I'll get by, I imagine, without any meatballs like you two. Pour me a drink, Franky."

Tony Castelli slapped her face soundly. "Meatballs, huh? That's what that goddamn Morey called me. I'll blast that bastard, if it's the last thing I ever do!"

"Better take him from behind, Tony," advised Lolly Durand.

Castelli gulped his drink, slapped her across the cheek again, and strode into the bathroom, yanking off his bloodstained coat and shirt.

"You must like to get belted around," Borchek grumbled, handing Lolly a drink. "Why don't you keep your trap shut? Tony's really teed off tonight."

"You boys brought me up rough, didn't you?" Lolly Durand said. "Maybe I like it that way."

Franky Borchek stared at her, and shook his shaggy blond head. "Dames," he growled. "If I live to be a hundred, I'll never be able to figure you dames out for a minute."

"Don't let it worry you, Franky," said Lolly. "We can't even figure ourselves out, most of the time. But take me now, I've got nothing more to lose, have I?"

"Your life maybe."

"And that don't matter a damn to me any more," Lolly Durand said.

Tony Castelli came out of the bathroom, combing his oily blue-black hair back in a long waving pompadour. "Come on, let's check out of this rathole. And take little Lolly to her nice new home in the country, where they sleep all day and work all night."

CHAPTER TEN

Life went on as usual at Ellinger's Escort Service. There was no word from Lolly Durand, no trace of Ann Norvill, and to date Duke Morey had been unable to spot any subversive activities in the organization. Duke was getting considerable daytime duty, because of his interest in sports and his reluctance to go all the way with clients who wanted amorous dalliance. This pleased and relieved him, and made the work more endurable. At the same time it made life harder, because he was getting that woman need real bad every morning and every night.

Jane Tolman called for him about once a week, and he generally spent his free evenings and his days off with her, their friendship ripening but their desires held in restraint and abeyance, ever since that one flare-up of passion, which Lolly Durand had interrupted. Although neither of them knew it, it was hell for the other after each date. Jane could hardly keep her knees together for a single hour some nights after Duke left.

Duke hoped for a call from Stella Leeds, because he wanted to learn about her true under-cover connection with Ellinger's, as well as what she might know concerning Ann Norvill. But Stella's name did not appear on his orders-for-the-day cards. A couple of times he was outside and off duty. Duke stopped at her apartment, but Stella was not at home.

Aware that Castelli and Borchek were probably gunning for him, Duke Morey kept an alert lookout for the two hoods, but they seemed to have vanished along with Lolly Durand. More and more, though, Duke found himself thinking of Jane's ripe body, her riper desire.

Since that night in front of the Village Barn, Gene Desmond and Park Lomax were cold and distant and vaguely hostile toward Duke, either ignoring him or eyeing him with malice and suspicion. That was all right with Duke. He had never cared for that pair, disliking Desmond in particular. He knew Gene hadn't forgiven him for finding that shoulder-holstered gun, and Duke wondered why anyone in this business should pack a pistol around.

The foppish be-mustached Payton Frappier became more obnoxious and revolting to Duke Morey from day to day, forever boasting about his sexual prowess and unique experiences with women. The suave cosmopolitan Rudy Valance, with his talk about Paris and other European capitals and the Riveria, was not much better, and Duke didn't like the cynical superior Clyde Vorse either. Sid Pawley wasn't a bad fellow, considering the social register and Princeton background that he was ostentatiously proud of, and there were other pretty good guys in the outfit. But none of them knew about Ann Norvill.

Next to Tom Garrick, Duke was fondest of big Bill Howell, the former Cornell fullback. They worked out in the gym, swam in the pool, talked football and sports in general, and argued good-naturedly about the Conference and the Ivy League.

The time came when Tom Garrick appeared to be unduly preoccupied and fretted by some worry, which he did not wish to discuss with his roommate.

One evening Duke was stretched out on a corner davenport in an empty darkened lounge, when Garrick and Gene Desmond paused just inside the doorway, in terse low-voiced debate.

"It's not my turn," Garrick said, protestingly.

"It's your duty, regardless of turn," declared Desmond. "You're the one she'll call for, Tom."

"Clyde Vorse has been out with her."

"She doesn't care for Vorse. She likes you."

"There'll be too much heat," Garrick said.

"That's for Ellinger to decide, not you. How many times has Horace been wrong?"

"There's always a first time. Her family's too big, Gene."

"You're still taking orders," Desmond said coldly. "There's no way out of this one, Garrick. It's your job, and you'll do it."

"I don't like it. There'll be hell to pay. It's too much of a risk." Garrick lit a cigarette, his face solemn and gaunted in the flare of the match.

"We're wasting time. Don't let that Morey make a rebel out of you, Tom. His turn's coming up before long, you know. He'll have to prove up—or take the consequences."

"Why are you so suspicious of Duke?" asked Tom Garrick.

"Something about him, I can't say exactly what." Gene Desmond smiled suddenly, and clapped Garrick on the back. "It's all set then? You're ready to operate, fellah?"

"I suppose so," Garrick said heavily.

They left the dim room, and Duke Morey lay there in the shadows for some time, pondering over what he had heard. Something big was coming up, and his roommate was involved in it—unwillingly. Ellinger's *was* more than just an escort bureau. Another girl was going to disappear, a girl from some prominent family, the same way Ann Norvill had vanished more than a year ago ...

The next day after lunch, Tom Garrick went directly to Ellinger's office, and Duke Morey returned to their room. He loaded a pipe and searched in vain for a match. There was a box of book-matches on Tom's chest-of-drawers. Duke went after a matchbook, and saw the instruction card lying there. He glimpsed the name, Louella Barnes, and stored it in his memory. Then, his pipe burning well, Duke left the room to look for Bill Howell, not wanting to be with Tom Garrick this afternoon.

The following day the newspapers had it: "LOUELLA BARNES, OIL HEIRESS, MISSING." There was a photograph of her, formal and glamorized. A picture of her father, and their palatial home in Oklahoma. Something must have gone wrong, Duke thought, to get this immediate publicity. Ellinger's machine had slipped a cog somewhere.

Duke Morey was in his easy chair reading the paper, when Tom Garrick came into the room and stood eyeing him and the newspaper narrowly. Duke motioned at the headlines. "Name's familiar, Tom. Haven't some of the boys been dating her?"

"I have, for one," Garrick said stiffly. "So what?"

"Nothing," Duke said mildly. "Just wondering if the cops will be around."

"They might," Garrick admitted. "But it won't do them any good. Ellinger's too big for them, Duke."

Duke Morey looked straight at him. "Tom, weren't you with Louella Barnes last night?"

Garrick's mouth tightened grimly. "You been snooping around, Duke? That's not a very healthy thing to do here."

"I wasn't snooping, but I saw your assignment card yesterday."

Tom Garrick sank down into the other large chair. "Yeah, I was with her. But I didn't kidnap her, if that's what you mean."

"You had something to do with it, Tom," said Duke gently.

"All right, so I did. But I'm clean. I'm covered all the way."

"That doesn't help Louella Barnes much. Or her family."

"She won't be hurt. Nothing's going to happen to her. She'll be back with her folks in a few days." Garrick made a tired gesture.

"Some money will change hands then," Duke Morey said.

"That has nothing to do with me—or with you," Tom Garrick said. "You'd better be careful, Duke. You don't know what you're up against here, boy."

"I'm beginning to, Tom."

Garrick leaned forward, elbows on knees, and bowed his brown crisp head burying his face in his big hands. "I shouldn't have got you into this, Duke," he mumbled through his fingers.

FORCED GIGOLOS

"I wanted to get in, Tom. Don't blame yourself for that. But I've been wondering about this business lately."

Garrick raised his strained face and sunken yellowish eyes. "Well, it's time you really knew something about it. You've been here long enough, Duke. I can tell you now, because you're slated for the next snatch yourself."

"What?" Duke Morey looked more perplexed than he was. "I'm slated for a snatch? I don't get it, Tom. What goes on here anyway?"

Garrick smiled thinly. "You'll get it, Duke. You'll find out. And you'll go through with it, whether you want to or not."

"Then Ellinger is in another business—under the surface?"

"He certainly is. Horace Ellinger wouldn't be in this for peanuts. He's big, Duke, bigger than anyone realizes."

"What's the pitch?"

"Kidnapping, blackmail, white-slaving, a combination of them all." Garrick's tone was bitter. "Usually the girl thinks she's in love and eloping. That's where we come in, but the ceremony never comes off. If her folks have money, they're asked to lay it on the line and keep quiet about it. They usually do both. If the girl is poor, she's sold to a call house or a brothel. They bring a good price, too." Garrick laughed hollowly.

"Why do the girls hold still for it? The poor ones, I mean."

"What they going to do, Duke? They're drugged and laid by five or six guys, time after time. They figure they're ruined, and they don't care what happens to themselves then. Instead of waking up married, they wake up in a whorehouse."

"What did you do to Louella Barnes, Tom?" asked Duke Morey.

"Nothing like that. I just slipped a mickey in her drink, and left her in a certain apartment," Tom Garrick said. "That's the only way I ever played it. We've got enough guys who enjoy the rape act."

"How did this one get in the papers so quick?"

77

"I don't know, Duke. But I had a hunch this one was going bad. Ellinger will fix it though. Nothing'll come of it."

Duke Morey shook his crewcut head. "And I'm supposed to pull a caper like that, Tom?"

"You'll have to," Garrick said. "There's no getting out of it—unless you want to die. Escorts disappear as well as girls, if they try to buck the big brass."

"What'll I have to do?"

"Not much. Just set up this girl for the snatch. Her family's in the chips, so it won't be a brothel case. If you can't make her fall, you slip something into her drink, and deliver her to some address. That's all, Duke. She passes out and you fade out. Someone else takes over, and that's the end of it so far as you're concerned. And Jane Tolman's old man pays off."

"*Jane Tolman?*" Duke Morey said, stark with horror. "If you think for a minute—"

Tom Garrick waved a weary hand. "I know, Duke. I used to feel that way myself. But you'll do it. You'll do it because you want to stay alive. If you don't, you'll drop out of sight yourself, and nobody'll ever find as much as a knucklebone of you! It has happened, Duke."

"But I couldn't do anything like that, Tom," said Duke Morey, his voice quivering with tension. "Not to Jane Tolman."

"It's out of your hands, Duke," said Tom Garrick, resignation and defeat in his voice. "From now on, until it's all over, you'll be a prisoner here. You'll be watched every second, and you won't communicate with anybody on the outside."

"They're framing me—or testing me. They know Jane Tolman is an old friend of mine."

"They're suspicious of you all right. For some reason, they'd like a chance to rub you out, Duke. I don't know why."

"They think I'm FBI or something?" Duke asked, forcing a laugh.

"Maybe they do. Whatever you are, Duke, you're in it up to your ears. And don't try to powder off or pull any doublecross. It'll be that much worse for you, if you do. They never get away, Duke, never ... Once you're in here, you aren't your own man any more. You're Horace Ellinger's man—if you can call it a man. And there's no way out of it—alive!" Tom Garrick sighed and slumped back in his chair.

"That's fantastic, Tom," said Duke. "You can't really believe that."

"I *know* it, Duke," said Garrick, with simple finality.

"It doesn't seem possible. An outfit like this, right in the heart of New York."

"It's incredible, but it's true. Period. I like you, Duke. I wouldn't give you a snow-job about this."

Duke Morey got up slowly. "Let's go down and get a drink, Tom. I need one."

"We'll bring a bottle back with us," Garrick said, smiling wanly. "I need a lot more than one, Duke."

Downstairs and outside the arched entrance of the barroom, Duke Morey saw two familiar figures at the bar, and halted with a restraining hand on Garrick's arm. "What the hell are those two doing here?"

Garrick followed his glance, and grimaced wryly. "Borchek and Castelli? They work for Ellinger too, Duke. Gunmen and strong-arm boys and under-cover agents. Specialists in the rape act I told you about. A couple of rare specimens. They don't show themselves much around here. They must've pulled off some successful deal for the company. Placed another well-broken-in blonde in some hook shop."

"How right you are," murmured Duke Morey. "You go ahead and get a bottle, Tom. I'll be waiting in the room. I had a little trouble with Castelli and Borchek. It's just as well if they don't see me here."

Duke Morey knew now why Ellinger and his lieutenants were suspicious of him, and why Desmond had hauled off Castelli in front of the Village Barn, and who to thank for putting the finger on Jane Tolman and himself... And what had become of Lolly Durand. There was no wealth behind her. Lolly was brothel bait, for sure.

Ann Norvill must have suffered the same fate as Lolly, he decided with a sick sinking sensation. They knew her family was rich, but they didn't know Ann had been disowned. So, instead of collecting ransom or blackmail, they had sold Ann into white slavery... They might better have killed her, he thought bitterly. Probably by now, Ann Norvill had done away with herself. But somebody was going to pay for that. A lot of people were going to pay for that and other things.

Sitting in the room, waiting for Garrick to come back with the whiskey, Duke Morey wondered how he could get hold of a gun. He should have bought one long ago. He had waited until it was too late... But he'd get hold of a gun somehow. And perhaps he could convert Tom Garrick to his side.

CHAPTER ELEVEN

Duke Morey came to know what it was like to be imprisoned in a gilded cage without bars. The illusion of freedom and normalcy made it more difficult to bear at times than strict confinement. He was neither incarcerated nor under armed guard, yet he was a prisoner, constantly watched and restricted, never alone. Both Duke and Tom Garrick were taken off active-duty status, and under orders from above Garrick became his shadow. It imposed a severe strain on both of them.

Duke was permitted no phone calls, no letters or wires, no communication whatsoever with the outside world. He knew Jane Tolman must be trying to get in touch with him, but her calls were not put through. And he had no means of warning Jane what Ellinger's had in store for her. It was a hopeless maddening situation. A thousand plans flashed and flickered through Duke Morey's mind, interwoven and twisted in writhing confusion, none of them logical or feasible upon analysis. He couldn't make a move until he was sent after Jane Tolman, and then it would be too late to save her. To trap the Ellinger outfit, Jane would have to be sacrificed, temporarily at least. The thought of that tormented Duke night and day, filled him with seething fury.

The newspapers heralded the return of Louella Barnes, the oil heiress, as Tom Garrick had predicted. It had all been a mistake, according to the story. She had simply been on a prolonged party with some friends on Long Island. Her father had flown to New York from Oklahoma, and there was a photograph of him with his daughter. Duke Morey wondered how much it had cost the old man, to save Louella from the disgrace of the compromising position she had been trapped into by Ellinger's Escort Service.

"You see, Duke," said Garrick. "Safe and sound, like I told you."

"Sure, because her father had the money to pay off," Duke said. "Even so, some of the boys might have taken advantage of her when she was knocked out. Some of our rapists like Castelli and Borchek."

Garrick shook his head. "They don't work the big jobs, Duke."

"Another break for the rich girls," Duke Morey said, thinking that Ann Norvill might have been turned over to those two hoodlums, after Ellinger learned that no large cash settlement was forthcoming from her family. He longed desperately to get his hands on a gun, but there didn't seem to be any chance of it.

Strained and distorted as the relations between Duke and Garrick were now, they contrived to avoid any outward show of feelings and to get along with a certain amount of harmony. In a way, Duke understood, Tom Garrick was as much a prisoner as he was ... They had grown close and fond of one another, before this came up, and Duke Morey hated to think that, when the crisis came, he might have to kill Garrick—if he could.

Some of the others were also keeping an eye on Duke Morey these days. Payton Frappier and Clyde Vorse were hanging around more than usual, while Park Lomax and Gene Desmond watched him coldly from a distance. Even the stocky Ben Zolnay and lank Rufus Kern took an aloof and morbid interest in Duke ... Sometimes Duke wondered if they had him tabbed for a federal agent, suspected Jane as his confederate, and plotted this course with deliberate and diabolical malice. But he doubted this, after sober consideration. They simply wanted to test him, make him as guilty as the rest. These were just the customary precautions taken with every new operator, preliminary to his first important assignment.

Duke Morey was briefed on the mission, first by Tom Garrick, then Desmond and Lomax, and finally by Rufus Kern and Ben Zolnay. It occurred to him that Horace Ellinger was seldom in sight about the establishment. Duke hadn't seen Ellinger since the first day he reported for work.

"You're going to be covered tight, Duke," warned Tom Garrick. "I hope you won't try to pull anything. You're a dead man, if you do."

"I don't want that girl hurt in any way, Tom," said Duke Morey.

"She won't be hurt. She'll just be held until arrangements are made with her father in Detroit."

"I don't see how Ellinger gets away with it."

"He's big, Duke," said Garrick. "He's got agents and influence and power everywhere."

"I wish I had a gun, Tom," said Duke.

"It wouldn't help you any. It'd just get you killed."

"Borchek and Castelli are out to get me."

"After this is over you can carry a gun, Duke."

"That may be too late."

"Where'd you meet up with them, anyway?" inquired Garrick.

Duke Morey smiled dimly. "Down in the village. Tangled with them three times. One night Castelli took a shot at me."

"What over, Duke?"

"I don't know what started it, at first. They just seemed to want to take me. Later we had trouble over a blonde they were rushing. A friend of Jane Tolman. They were feeding her reefers and probably heroin. Now they've put her away somewhere."

"They're a couple of low grade bastards," Tom Garrick said.

Duke Morey nodded his tawny head. "Get me an automatic, Tom."

"I can't, Duke. Not until this deal's finished. Castelli and Borchek won't dare to hit you until that's over."

"Are you going to spend your life in this rotten racket, Tom?"

"Not hardly, Duke. I'll break away one of these days," Garrick said, but there wasn't much hope or conviction in his tone, or in his amber eyes and grave face.

"That'll mean leaving New York."

"That's all right with me. I've had enough of it. I may go back into the Air Force anyway."

"You'd back me in a showdown against Castelli and Borchek, wouldn't you?"

"You're damn right, Duke," said Tom Garrick. "Or against Desmond and Lomax or any of them."

"That's good to hear, Tom," said Duke Morey, with a slow smile. "That makes me feel a lot better, boy."

"I don't like this business any better than you do, Duke," said Garrick. "But I'm in it a great deal deeper."

"When's this kidnap act coming off, Tom?" asked Duke.

"The next time Jane Tolman calls for you," Garrick said glumly.

It was all set, cold and precise in Duke Morey's brain. He would pick Jane Tolman up and take her to the Club Rivoli, and then deliver her to Number 123 in the Parkmont Apartments, preferably under the influence of knockout drops inserted in her last drink. That was all he had to do, before reporting back to the agency. He'd probably be under Ellinger guns every step of the evening, never really alone with her. Duke had to figure something out and have it ready...

The next time Jane Tolman called for him.

CHAPTER TWELVE

One dark glowering afternoon, Duke Morey and Tom Garrick were playing pool on an arc-lighted green table in an otherwise empty recreation room, when Zolnay and Kern entered.

"Sorry to intrude, gentlemen," Ben Zolnay said gutturally, rubbing at his beaked nose and jutting jaw. "But an emergency has arisen, and we are caught short-handed at the moment. A certain young lady we are interested in has just been reported missing from her—uh—place of employment. Borchek and Castelli think they can apprehend her, before she does any damage. We want two men to follow and cover them, although Franky and Tony claim they won't need any cover. You gentlemen seem to be the only two available."

"Anything to break the monotony," Tom Garrick said, racking his cue stick.

"Right," agreed Duke. "But Borchek and Castelli aren't very fond of me."

Rufus Kern scratched his brush of reddish hair, lean angular face frowning. "They got a job to do. So have you. Personal feelings won't enter into this. Go to your room and get your hats and coats. No time to waste. The other two boys are waiting in the garage."

The windows of their room were gray and streaming, as they took light raincoats and old hats from their closets. Rufus Kern rapped briskly and came in, thin and towering, to hand them each a shoulder-holster with an automatic pistol. "We don't want any gunplay, but we got to play it safe," Kern said, in his clipped harsh voice. "You both been in the service and handled guns." Removing their sport jackets, Duke and Tom adjusted the holsters and slung the pistols under their left armpits. Duke was already wondering how he could retain possession of this precious weapon, until his date with Jane came up.... Before they went out, Kern drew Garrick aside and spoke to him in an undertone. *Warning Tom to watch me like a hawk,* Duke thought.

In the company garage, Tony Castelli and Franky Borchek were sitting in a black sedan smoking cigars, with Tony at the wheel. They grinned at the sight of Duke and Garrick, and Castelli said: "Your blonde friend Lolly has busted loose, Morey. You're goin' to help us pick her up and plant her back in that whorehouse. How you like that?"

Duke Morey shrugged silently, content to wait until it was time to act, the weight of the pistol reassuring under his left arm.

Borchek said: "A coupla patsies they give us for cover. If a gun went off, them two pretty boys'd never stop runnin'."

"You two might be able to handle one girl—without shooting her," Duke Morey said. "But it's doubtful."

"Cut it out," Tom Garrick said tersely. "Where you heading first?"

"The Village," Castelli said. "She'll go there. If she don't run to the cops first."

"Let's go," Garrick said, climbing in behind the wheel of the second black sedan, with Duke getting in beside him. Castelli blew his horn and the wide door slid open, and the two cars rolled out into the rain and the traffic. Tom Garrick handled the machine with casual expertness, and Duke thought he must have been a good pilot.

"Like getting out of jail, Tom," said Duke.

"Yeah, except we aren't really out," Garrick said. "This is the girl you spoke of, eh? Jane Tolman's friend?"

Duke Morey nodded, thumbing back his hat. "I don't know if I'll let them take her back or not."

"Have to shoot them to stop 'em, Duke."

"What's bad about that?" Duke asked quietly.

"Nothing much," Garrick admitted. "If we could clear ourselves with Ellinger."

"I never fired at a man, except in combat," Duke Morey said. "But I wouldn't mind blasting those two."

"Always hated their guts myself. But I don't see how we can get away with it, Duke."

"Something will break, Tom."

"They're supposed to be pretty hot with the rods."

"I'll risk that," Duke said. "There's plenty of yellow in those two tramps."

Rain slashed at the windshield and windows, the wipers swinging to and fro in cleansing arcs, and raindrops drummed and danced on the pavement. Low-hanging clouds shrouded the higher buildings, and lights shimmered through the premature darkness of mid-afternoon. Vari-colored umbrellas bloomed and bobbed along the sidewalks, and unsheltered pedestrians walked with bent heads and hunched shoulders. Driving skilfully, Tom Garrick kept behind the first black sedan, and Duke Morey pondered on the problem of eliminating Castelli and Borchek without putting themselves on the spot at Ellinger's Escort Service. The answers, if any, were slow in coming.

Washington Square was deserted for once, sodden and desolate under the rain, the lighted show-windows of the little bookstores and art shops shining in the grayness. Castelli pulled in before Jane Tolman's apartment house, and Garrick parked in back of him. Duke wished he could get to see Jane, but there wasn't much chance of it. Motioning them to stay in the car, Castelli and Borchek went into the building. They were back shortly, alone, and Borchek said: "Nobody home. We'll try some other places."

They stopped at several more apartment houses, which Duke wasn't familiar with, and then they began to hit the taverns and bars, with no better success. Finally Castelli swung into the curb near the mouth of the alley beside the Cabana Club, where Duke had first become involved with the two hoodlums, and Garrick found an open space a couple of cars ahead. Once more Borchek signaled them to remain behind, but Duke Morey said, "To hell with them," and threw the door open and got out, with Garrick climbing out on the other side. Castelli and Borchek glared but said nothing, swaggering toward the entrance.

The neon sign was already glowing, staining the misty gloom crimson and green, and the sad tinkling music of Clift's piano met them in the corridor. Lolly Durand was there, alone in a booth by the far wall, changed so shockingly that Duke scarcely recognized her. She had aged and coarsened beyond belief, all the youth and freshness beaten out of her, a strained wild look about the big blue eyes and painted mouth. A spasm of fear crossed her face at the sight of Castelli and Borchek. She started, as if to rise and run for it, then sank back into the booth with a despairing gesture, as they strode toward her.

Duke Morey and Tom Garrick stopped at the bar. Manahan had just come on duty, in a clean crisp white jacket, his hard broken-nosed features easing into a broad smile as he saw who it was. "Hiyuh, Duke. How's tricks?"

"Not bad, Man," said Duke, ordering a double scotch for Garrick and bourbon for himself, and placing a bill on the polished wood. "Expense account this time."

"You're working, huh? That's fine, Duke. Heard anything from Ann?"

"Not a whisper, Man. Has Jane been in lately?"

Manahan shook his bald head. "Not since she was here with you." He nodded at the booth, in which Castelli and Borchek were now sitting with the blonde girl. "Lolly was looking for Jane, too. What the hell's happened to Lolly? She been on the weed or something?"

"I guess so, Manny. How long's she been in here?"

"All afternoon, they tell me. She ought to be drunk, but it don't seem to hit her. I knew she was headed for skid row when she started playing around with them two monkeys."

"You couldn't tell her anything, Man," said Duke. "She had to learn the hard way."

They sipped their drinks and smoked cigarettes, while Borchek and Castelli drank and talked with Lolly Durand, who no longer registered fear or anything but dull apathy. When Garrick went to the men's room, Duke leaned across the bar and spoke to Manahan:

"Get this word to Jane for me, Man. Tell her to bring a gun the next time she goes out with me."

"You in a jam, Duke?"

"Not yet. I just want to be heeled, in case something comes up."

"I'll tell her, Duke," promised Manahan. "I hope you aren't getting into anything too deep."

"Nothing like that, Manny."

"You had any more trouble with them two crumbs?"

Duke glanced at Castelli and Borchek. "Not to speak of, Man. But we're keeping an eye on them today."

"You need a heater right now then," Manahan declared earnestly.

"Got one I borrowed for the day," Duke Morey told him.

Garrick returned and bought a round, and Duke introduced him to Manahan, who set up the third round while they talked baseball and boxing and horse-racing. By that time Castelli and Borchek had Lolly on her feet, paying the waiter and escorting her to the exit into the alley. Duke and Garrick said so long to Manahan and trailed after them, with Man calling, "Take care of yourself, boys."

Rain filtered into the alley, darkening Lolly Durand's yellow hair, as she drooped unsteadily between the two men.

"You can run along home now," Tony Castelli said.

Tom Garrick shook his head. "We've got orders to cover you all the way, Tony."

"We don't need no goddamn boy scouts coverin' us," Franky Borchek said, spitting disgustedly at the brick wall.

"You aren't running the show yet," Duke Morey said. "Move along."

Lolly Durand's head jerked up, her glazed blue eyes staring at Duke. "*You?*" she cried, laughing hysterically. "You mixed up in this, too? Oh my God, what next?" Her laughter rose crazily, and Castelli raised a hand to cuff her.

"Don't do it, meatball," said Duke Morey.

Castelli's black liquid eyes blazed at Duke with pure venom and hatred, but he dropped his hand and yanked Lolly along toward the street, mumbling profanely under his breath.

"Where you going from here?" Garrick asked, on the sidewalk.

"Follow us and find out," Borchek growled.

"Don't think I can't," Garrick said. "Come on, Duke."

They piled into the sedan and waited until Castelli pulled out and passed them, swinging out then and hanging tight on the tail of the other car. Castelli tried to lose them in the traffic, but Garrick drove with reckless daring skill to stick with him, and after a time Tony gave it up and the pace was easier. Through the rain Duke could dimly see the blonde head of Lolly Durand between the broad-shouldered bulks of the two men.

"Heading for a North River ferry to Jersey," Tom Garrick guessed aloud. "Christopher Street maybe."

"Hope so," Duke Morey murmured. "On a ferry in this storm, we might get a chance at them."

"You still thinking of taking them, Duke?"

"I'm not letting them take that kid back to—*that*," Duke said, with slow emphasis. "She can be saved now, Tom. A few months more and she'll be gone for good."

"I know, Duke," said Garrick, miserably. "But how we going to square it with Ellinger?"

"I'll think of something."

"Nobody tailing us, is there?"

"No, I've been watching for that, Tom," said Duke Morey. It was raining harder than ever now, with flares of lightning splitting the sky in jagged blue and greenish-white streaks, and thunder toppling and crashing among the skyscrapers. Rain-dazzled lights glistened everywhere, and laid broken javelins of all colors across streaming automobiles and the slick dark pavement. Endless hordes of humanity swarmed in under the downpour, which softened and muted the racketing din of the city streets. Neon signs flowed in lurid jittering patterns, flashing on and off, and great display windows gleamed with unreal splendour. Bright-colored taxis raced through the clogged thoroughfares, and horns clamored incessantly on all sides. Duke Morey, taut and brittle with mounting tension, was glad that Tom Garrick was driving.

As Tom had predicted, they came to a halt in the ranked waiting automobiles on the pier of the Christopher Street ferry, inching forward onto the parking deck after the huge craft unloaded. They had lost the other car in this final confusion, but they knew it was on board somewhere. Many people crawled out of their cars and made for the lights and sheltered warmth of congested passenger cabins, but Garrick and Duke waited in their sedan until the ferry wheeled ponderously away from the dock. Gulls swooped in the gusty rainswept darkness, and Duke rolled down his window to feel the sharp salty whip of the wind on his fevered face. Behind them rose the fabulous towers of Manhattan, brilliant with millions of lighted windows, weirdly illuminated now and then by vivid lightning flashes, the thunder rumbling and echoing like artillery fire in the distance. They peered around the close-packed cars in search of the other black sedan, while the rain pattered on the roof and blurred the windshield and windowglass.

Duke Morey took the automatic out from beneath his left arm. It was a short .38 Colt, good enough for close work. He removed and checked the clip, replaced it and eased off the safety and put the gun in the right-hand pocket of his raincoat. "I'm going to take a look, Tom," he said evenly. "It's my show. You can sit it out, if you want to."

Tom Garrick grinned and shook his head, inspecting his own pistol. "The last thing Kern told me was to keep close watch of you, Duke. I'll go along with you."

As they got out into the windtorn rain, forked lightning splintered the whole sky with an unearthly violet-hued glare, and thunder boomed and reverberated over land and water. They prowled through the abandoned cars on the open deck, ducking into the lashing downpour and looking for the machine that held Lolly Durand and Tony Castelli and Franky Borchek, walking with their hands on the guns in their topcoat pockets.

CHAPTER THIRTEEN

They found the Ellinger sedan parked near the rail, with Lolly Durand alone in the front seat, huddled abjectly, her blonde head hanging. Duke Morey looked around with care, but the two hoodlums were not in sight, nothing moved in that vicinity of the rain-scourged deck. He opened the door on Lolly's side, and she lifted her head with an effort.

"You want to go back to that place, Lolly?" he asked.

"What difference does it make? I'm going."

"Not necessarily."

"Told me I'd never get away," Lolly mumbled. "Guess they was right." She gazed blankly at Duke. "Didn't know you was one of 'em, Duke. And you always preaching to me."

"I'm not one of 'em," Duke Morey said. "We're going to take you home, Lolly."

Lolly Durand laughed insanely. "Home? ... Beat it, sonny boy, before they come back and throw you to the fishes. They're probably watching from somewhere right now. Go 'way, leave me alone."

"You *want* to go back to that house?"

"Maybe I belong there. What is it to you anyway? Blow, brother, I don't feel like talking." She gestured weakly.

Duke studied her tense features and dilated eyes. "You're charged up again, Lolly."

She laughed again. "So what? Just one little heroin capsule Tony gave me. Go peddle your peanuts, fade out, jump in the river!"

"You like the kind of life you've been leading?" Duke asked patiently, aware that Garrick was standing watch at his back.

"God, no!" moaned Lolly Durand, shaking her head violently. "But it's too late, Duke. I'm all washed up."

"No, you aren't, Lolly. You can be saved—if you want to try. We'll take you back to Jane Tolman."

Lolly spread her palms. "She wouldn't let me in the place."

"You know Jane better than that. She wants to help you."

"No, they'll kill you, Duke. You'll just get yourself killed. Get out of here while you can." Lolly Durand waved him away, and slammed the door shut.

Behind him Tom Garrick said, "Here they come, Duke," and he saw Castelli and Borchek striding toward them in the wind-blown rain, as lightning flared with eerie blinding brilliance and thunder volleyed with a broken jarring roar.

"What the hell you doin' here?" Tony Castelli demanded. "Get back to your own car." He skirted the front of the sedan, moving toward the driver's seat.

"You heard the man," Franky Borchek said, shouldering Garrick aside and elbowing Duke roughly away from the car. He was opening the door, when Duke Morey drew and chopped the gun butt down on the back of his head. Borchek sagged, his crumpled hat falling off and his shaggy blond hair flying awry. Duke struck again, as Borchek grunted and spun slowly away from the door, driving him back and down by the right rear wheel, rolling once and lying still.

Tony Castelli was reaching under his left arm, his motion quick and practiced, but Tom Garrick was already lifting his pistol from his raincoat pocket. Flame speared across the shining black hood at Castelli, the report lost in a crash of thunder, and Tony fell back against the front fender of the next car, his own gun clearing and jetting fire over the hood.

Tom Garrick had dropped and glass shattered somewhere behind them, and Duke Morey was pressed tight against the side of the sedan, when Garrick's automatic started hammering down below as he shot underneath the car at Castelli's legs. Bullets screeched against metal, and Tony Castelli swore and went down thrashing on the wet deck.

Duke Morey turned to the rear and glimpsed Franky Borchek coming around and up on his knees and left hand, the pistol in his right fist coming to bear. Duke squeezed the trigger twice, the gun blazing and jumping in his hand, and Borchek lurched back, back again from the solid impacts on his broad chest. Blue-green lightning etched the rain-soaked scene, as Franky Borchek fell on his shoulders, squirmed over kicking onto his riddled chest, and stretched out motionless on the drenched boards.

Duke Morey looked around the panic, sick and shuddering all over with the abrupt reaction, but nobody was rushing in their direction, no one seemed to have heard the shooting with that thunderstorm raging about the ferry. Tom Garrick was up beside him, slitted eyes sweeping the car-lined deck, and Lolly Durand was slumped low in the front seat, face hidden in tense clawed hands.

"You all right, Tom?" asked Duke.

Garrick nodded. "Lucky, I guess." He went around the front of the sedan to make sure of Tony Castelli, and Duke dragged Borchek's dead bulk toward the rail. Garrick turned to him. "What we going to do with 'em, Duke?"

"Dump 'em overboard," Duke Morey said. "It's the only way, Tom."

Garrick came to lend a hand with Borchek, and they heaved him overboard and down into the watery darkness. They paused beside Castelli's body until the lightning dimmed out, then hauled him to the rail and over the side after his partner, with a thunderbolt shaking the wet deck under their shoes.

"What's our story, Duke?" panted Garrick, letting the rain wash his bloody hands and wiping them on his raincoat.

"We lost them, after they picked up the girl," Duke Morey said. "They ran away from us in traffic. We don't know where they went, or anything about it." He noticed dark stains on his own hands, and rinsed them in the steady downpour.

"If they should find her, we're done for," Garrick said grimly.

Duke nodded, water streaming from his hatbrim. "Have to keep her out of sight. Get her out of town. Jane'll take care of that, Tom."

"I hope so. What'll we do now?"

"Stay right on the ferry and ride back across," Duke Morey said. "In our car. We leave this one right where it is."

"Too bad we can't ditch it in the river. The guns too ... But we've got to turn them in, cleaned and reloaded."

Duke Morey pulled the car door open and lifted Lolly Durand outside. "Come on, baby, we're taking the other car. We're going home."

The sobbing girl supported between them, they walked back through the massed automobiles and got into their sedan, Lolly in the middle of the broad front seat, her damp head on Duke's wet shoulder, her body quivering as she wept without sound. Drying his hands on a handkerchief, Duke got out a pack of cigarettes and Tom Garrick flicked his lighter. Inhaling deeply, they settled back to wait, as the ferry wallowed in toward the Jersey shore.

The unloading, the wait at the wharf and the loading, the slow cruise back across the rain-lashed river, seemed to take an eternity. Duke Morey was still waiting for somebody to come after them, arrest them for murder. Even in that storm, it was difficult to believe that the gunfight and killing had gone unseen and unheard ... But nobody came, nothing happened.

Lolly Durand had stopped crying and regained some of her composure, sitting up straight between them now and smoking a cigarette.

"You'll have to keep out of sight, Lolly, or leave town at once," Duke told her. "If you don't—if you're seen around—we're liable to get killed."

"I will, Duke, I'll do anything," she said. "I'll never be able to thank you enough or pay you back."

"You don't owe us anything, Lolly," said Duke. "We did it because we wanted to. Just straighten up now, kid, and lay off the liquor and the hay, and be a good girl again."

"Do you think I can, Duke?"

"Sure, you can. It won't be easy, at first, but you can do it."

"But you don't know what I've been through," Lolly Durand said.

Duke patted her shoulder. "I can imagine, Lolly. You've got to forget all that."

"The first part of it—before I even went—went to work—was the worst. That Castelli and Borchek—I'm *glad* they're dead!" Lolly shivered deeply. "The men over there—they were rough and crude and mostly drunk, but they weren't too bad. At least, they weren't teaheads or junkies. They treated you pretty decent. Some of 'em real nice and gentle, even drunk, you'd be surprised... I guess, if they'd all been like Tony and Franky, I'd be in the nuthouse by now."

"Most men are fairly decent," Duke said soothingly.

"I think so, Duke. I've got to think so."

"But you want to be careful hereafter, kid."

"I will be, don't worry. I guess I'm plenty dumb, Duke, but not dumb enough to ever go for any more coked-up gangsters."

Back in the endless rushing roar of New York, the rain was slowing and the thunder and lightning had ceased, as they crept in line off the ferry and rode across toward the Village. Jane Tolman's apartment was unlighted, apparently still empty, but Lolly had kept her key, and she unlocked the door for them and switched on some lights. Duke Morey was disappointed, and beginning to be afraid that something might have happened to Jane Tolman.

He poured a round of brandies, which they all needed, and they debated what to do next. Duke and Tom would have to get back to Ellinger's before long, and they were both dreading it.

"Perhaps we ought to make our break right now, Duke," said Garrick.

"If we did, they'd know we got Castelli and Borchek, Tom," said Duke. "And they'd never rest until they ran us down."

Garrick nodded his brown head, amber eyes solemn and brooding. "You're right, Duke. We'll have to go back and face it."

"They won't find the bodies for a while—perhaps not ever," Duke Morey mused. "I'd like to bust the whole outfit, Tom, now that we've started.

"I wouldn't mind either. But it's too much of a job for two men."

"Yeah, it is. We could swing it, with police help, but I don't know just how...I'm not thinking very sharp tonight." Duke drained his glass, and reached for the bottle of Hennessey's Three Star.

When Tom Garrick excused himself to go to the bathroom, Duke Morey turned to the blonde girl. "Get this straight, Lolly. Go to the cops with your story. The first part of it, forget about tonight. How you were forced into that house, how you escaped, and that stuff. After that have Jane call me for a date, and tell her to bring a gun in her bag." He handed her the telephone pad and pencil. "Write this down, Lolly Parkmont Apartments, Number 123, on Central Park West. The night Jane goes out with me, have the police cover that address. Tell them they're planning to snatch Jane, the way they did you."

"Are they, Duke?" she asked, in terror.

"Yes, but I'll see that they don't get her," Duke said. "Have you got it, Lolly? You'd better ask for police protection, and be with the cops the night they go to the Parkmont. Tell them to let me go, and close in on the men who follow us to that apartment. I've got to take Jane there and leave her, see?"

"I see, I've got it," Lolly murmured. "But I'm awful scared, Duke."

"Nothing to worry about—now," said Duke. "Put that address away, Lolly. And explain everything to Jane, as well as you can."

She nodded and tucked the slip of paper into the bodice of her dress, and Duke Morey returned to contemplating his glass, as Tom Garrick emerged, hands and face scrubbed clean, brown hair neatly combed.

"We ought to be going, Duke," said Garrick, glancing at his platinum wrist-watch.

"I know it, Tom. Hate to leave Lolly alone, but I guess we'll have to. Whatever you do, Lolly, don't go out until Jane comes back."

"I won't," Lolly Durand said. "I'll be okay, Duke. I can call in one of the girls down the hall to stay with me—until Jane comes."

"Attagirl," said Duke. "You're going to be all right. Everything's going to be fine."

"I—I want to thank you boys again," Lolly said. "But there aren't any words for it … And Duke, there's something else. I—I hate to tell you this, but you—you ought to know it. I saw Ann Norvill."

"Where?" Duke asked, the sickness and the horror already starting inside him.

"In that—that house, where they put me. Oh God, it was awful, awful! … Poor Ann, poor poor Ann."

"I was beginning to expect that," Duke Morey said, dull and lifeless, his face drawn to the bone, his gray eyes stricken and hopeless. "How is she, Lolly?"

"Bad, Duke, bad. So terribly changed—and lost. She—she didn't know me, at first. Then she didn't—didn't want me to tell you or Jane or anybody. But I had to, Duke, I had to!" Her blue eyes brimmed with tears.

"Of course, you had to. You did right to tell me, Lolly."
Reaching for the pad and pencil, Duke asked: "Where is that
house?"

Lolly named the town, and gave him the street address,
"Twelve-sixty Brushwood."

Duke wrote it down and thanked her. "Well, we're on our
way, Lolly. Better call your friend in. And don't worry, don't be
afraid."

"I'll be all right, Duke," said Lolly Durand. "And you—don't
you go do anything crazy now, Duke."

"I won't," Duke promised. "Keep your chin up, gal."

"Good night, Lolly," said Tom Garrick gently.

They went out and walked toward the head of the stairs,
and Duke Morey glanced up at the starred bullet-hole Castelli
had put in the ceiling, and tried to realize that Tony Castelli and
Franky Borchek were dead and gone, drowned deep in the North
River and drifting toward the Atlantic Ocean ... And tried not to
think about Ann Norvill, wasted and wrecked in that brothel on
the other side of the river, lost forever, deader than Castelli and
Borchek.

Looking at his companion, Garrick thought Duke's gray eyes
had darkened to bitter green depths. He said, "Ann Norvill. You
asked me about her once, Duke. I couldn't tell you—then."

"What about her, Tom?"

"Gene Desmond set her up for the take, Gene and Park
Lomax. When they found out the family wasn't going to pay off,
they turned her over to Borchek and Castelli. I think Vorse and
Frappier had a hand in it, too."

"Thanks," Duke said tautly. "That's all I need to know."

CHAPTER FOURTEEN

There wasn't any alarm over the failure of Castelli and Borchek to return to Ellinger's that night. Kern and Zolnay saw no reason to doubt the story told by Duke and Garrick, that the other two had picked up the girl and ducked out of sight with her. Ellinger's subordinates knew the two hoods, knew they hadn't wanted the cover of Duke and Tom in the first place. It was quite possible that Castelli and Borchek had decided to romp the night away with Lolly Durand, before depositing her back at 1260 Brushwood.

The automatics had been cleaned, the clips refilled, before they were turned in to Rufus Kern, and Duke Morey and Tom Garrick retired with a sense of vast relief and some hopeful security.

But the next day was altogether different. The brothel on Brushwood reported that Lolly Durand had not been returned. Then the company sedan was discovered abandoned on that ferry boat, without a trace of Tony Castelli and Franky Borchek.

The inquisition began at once, with Duke Morey and Tom Garrick being questioned, together and separately, all afternoon and far into the night. First Desmond and Lomax worked on them, with Kern and Zolnay conducting the next cross-examination, and finally they were brought before Horace Ellinger himself. But they stuck to their story, refused to break or even crack, and the officers of the bureau had nothing to pin on them.

It was an ordeal, however, that strained raw fretted nerves to the limit and beyond. At two in the morning, Duke Morey lay fully dressed on his bed, while Tom Garrick was sweating out another third-degree in Ellinger's office. Park Lomax came after Duke again, smiling and drawling pleasantly, and Duke stumbled wearily after him to the inner sanctum.

Horace Ellinger peered up at him from behind the desk, bulbous eyes magnified by the horn-rimmed glasses, bristling large head tilted, broad bloated face, fish-belly white except for the blue jowls. "No use in lying any further, Morey," he said, in mild cultured tones. "Garrick broke down and confessed everything. You killed Borchek and Castelli, and sunk their bodies in the river. All we want to know from you now, is why you joined this agency in the first place. Who are you working for, Morey?"

"I'm not working for anybody—but you."

"Why did you kill those two men then?"

"We didn't."

"Garrick says you did."

"If he said that, he lied. You must have tortured it out of him."

Horace Ellinger smiled. "We haven't resorted to any such methods as yet. Unfortunately we may have to, unless you start telling the truth, Morey. You have nothing to gain by any more lying, my boy. Garrick told us everything, but we want to hear it from you, too. We might even forgive you for killing them, if you'd explain why you did it."

"There's nothing to explain. I didn't do it."

"Garrick did it alone?"

"Nobody did anything," Duke said.

It went on and on, the same relentless questions over and over again, beating at him in the bright hot light until Duke was ready to burst out screaming. When Ellinger grew tired, Zolnay and Kern took over, crowding in and shooting their questions, and after a while Desmond and Lomax resumed the grilling, Desmond leaning over Duke, heckling and badgering, threatening and shaking his fist in Duke's haggard sweaty face.

But Duke Morey refused to be caught or crossed up or shaken from his original story, and finally they gave up in disgust and sent him shambling back to his room, stunned and dazed and groggy with nausea. Tom Garrick was not there. Duke undressed with numb blundering fingers and fell into bed, too exhausted to rest or sleep. Too filled with fury and hatred for Desmond and Lomax and the entire Ellinger outfit, and hollow with despair for Ann Norvill. With daylight graying the windows, he finally fell into fitful slumber ...

The room was flooded with sunshine when Tom Garrick came in, sunken-eyed and hollow-cheeked, to wake him up. "Jane Tolman called. It's set for tonight, Duke. They're going to lay off and let us go through with this one." He handed over the assignment card.

Blinking at it with dull crusted eyes, Duke Morey suddenly jerked upright in bed, as he observed the switch in directives. He was to take Jane to the Valencia Gardens, instead of the Club Rivoli, and deliver her to the Fenwick Apartments, Number 221, on Madison, instead of the Parkmont on Central Park West. That made all his instructions to Lolly Durand and the police invalid and useless.

"What's the idea of these changes, Tom?"

Garrick shrugged. "They often do that, Duke. Especially when their agent has been exposed to the outside world, like you were the other day. Just to make sure that nothing leaks out, you know."

"The bastards think of everything, don't they?" Duke muttered.

"They don't miss much," Tom Garrick admitted ruefully.

"Are you going out tonight, Tom?"

"Sure, I'll be at the Valencia. You're going to have lots of company, Duke. Make your debut in real style. Limousine, chauffeur, bodyguard, everything."

"How delightful," Duke Morey said, with gentle irony, thinking that everything had gone wrong, and there was no way, no time, to correct any part of it. He had gambled and lost, lost for Jane Tolman as well as himself. That was the worst phase of it. He wasn't in it alone.

They had him buttoned up tight all right. Duke recalled Ellinger's query as to whom he worked for. They might suspect him of being some kind of federal agent, but they knew he had another and more personal reason for being here. Lolly Durand must have mentioned his relationship with the missing Ann Norvill to Borchek and Castelli, and they naturally had relayed the information to headquarters. No wonder Ellinger was suspicious of him. No wonder they were putting him to the test with Jane Tolman.

Well, if Jane brought that gun and he could get hold of it, Duke Morey was going to try and make some sorts of a break and a fight for it, regardless of the odds. He had got Jane into this. He couldn't leave her helpless in their foul hands, even though it cost him his life … Life didn't seem so important, since he had learned the true fate of Ann Norvill.

If he had to die, in order to save Jane from a similar tragedy, Duke was resolved to go under fighting, and take as many of them as possible along with him. He wanted to get Gene Desmond and Park Lomax, for certain, and Clyde Vorse and Payton Frappier also. And the Big Three—Ellinger and Kern and Zolnay—if he lasted long enough.

Tom Garrick got dressed first and left the room without comment, his fine straight features more somber and gaunt than ever. Duke was making leisurely preparations for his toilet when Tom came back, and Duke was almost positive that his roommate now wore a shoulder-holstered gun under the loose-fitting coat of his handsome brown gabardine suit.

Duke Morey shaved and showered and dressed with elaborate care, putting on a dark gray flannel suit with a narrow bright-striped tie, knotted perfectly into the round collar of his fresh white shirt and held with a gold pin, an inch of white French cuffs and gold links showing at his strong tanned wrists. He looked pretty good, considering what he'd been through and had on his mind, he thought, as he gave his close-cut sandy hair a final brushing, the lights gilding his head with bronze. He looked fine, but he felt like hell inside.

When the time came Duke went through into the company garage and saw the great gleaming town car waiting there, with a chauffeur at the wheel and suave smiling Rudy Valance beside him as armed escort. They were going to see that he had no time alone with Jane Tolman tonight ... The long limousine resembled a hearse, Duke Morey thought, as he walked toward it, and that's exactly what it might turn out to be for him this evening.

CHAPTER FIFTEEN

At the shabby old apartment house in the Village, a crowd of noisy children and oddly-attired bohemian characters gathered about the big polished car. Duke Morey got out with a vague feeling of guilt, embarrassment and shame, but Rudy Valance, stepping from the front seat with a lordly air, plainly enjoyed this curious attention.

"Live brave and hope high, children of the proleteriat," said Rudy Valance. "You too may ride and dwell in luxury, barring an atomic war and taxes." He mounted the worn musty stairway at Duke's side, ignoring Duke's glance of distaste as they waited outside of Jane Tolman's door. She opened it, small and dainty and smartly tailored, her brown head tilted high, brown eyes masking their surprise at the sight of Duke's overdressed companion.

Duke Morey introduced them soberly, refused Jane's offer of a drink, and escorted her outside, with Valance close at their heels.

"Well, well, we're riding in style tonight," Jane Tolman said, as she saw the limousine. "I'll be a marked woman in this neighborhood."

"Yeah, I got promoted," Duke said dryly. "I'm a big operator now."

Rudy Valance bowed to Jane. "Your chic petite loveliness would mark you in any company, madamoiselle."

"Why, thank you," Jane murmured. "You're very gallant indeed."

There was no privacy, no chance of talking in the car, with those four ears cocked up front. Jane, sitting at the right, was somewhat startled when Duke suddenly grasped her in his arms and drew her close. Feeling as foolish and awkward as a school-boy on his first date, Duke Morey held her tight and kissed her hard on the mouth. Jane returned the embrace, her right arm around him, her hidden left hand busy in her bag. "The gun?" he whispered, against her lips, and Jane moved her head up and down, her left hand in the right pocket of his coat now. "There," she murmured, mouth moving against his, and he felt the compact weight of the automatic, as Jane withdrew her hand behind the screen of their enwrapped figures.

"Call the police?" Duke asked, under his breath.

"Twenty-fifth Precinct. Lolly's with them."

Which won't do us a damn bit of good, Duke thought, because Ellinger pulled a change-up pitch on us, and we're hit-ting Madison instead of Central Park West. I'll have to get to a phone somehow ... "Don't worry, Janie," he said, and was draw-ing away from her, when Rudy Valance called laughingly from the front seat: "Break it up, Morey. You're making me ravenously hungry."

"Sorry, Rudy," said Duke. "But I haven't seen this little girl for a long time."

"The night is young," Valance said. "Hours pour l'amour ahead of you young lovers. You Americans are too rash and impetuous, unappreciative of the delights of anticipation."

When they got out under the blue-and-gold lighted marquee of the Valencia Gardens, Tom Garrick was waiting there on the curb, tall and debonair in brown gabardine. Garrick shook hands with Duke, acknowledged the introduction to Jane Tolman, and insisted on their joining him at the table he had reserved. The gun felt heavy and bulging on Duke's right hip, and he walked with his hands thrust casually into jacket pockets, aware of the eyes of the chauffeur and Valance on his high broad back.

In the dim smoky interior, Garrick had a ringside table and ordered drinks, and when the glasses were empty he asked Jane to dance, with Duke's kind permission. As they glided away into the shadowy throng of dancers, Duke Morey leaned back in his chair and wondered where Garrick's loyalty lay in this affair. Which side would Tom take, when the showdown came? ... Searching the perimeter of the dance floor, he caught fleeting glimpses of the foppish Payton Frappier and stern Clyde Vorse, blond quiet Park Lomax and the big darkly handsome Gene Desmond. The Ellinger Escort Service was well represented tonight, and every exit covered.

When Duke Morey started dancing with Jane, hoping for a few minutes of private conversation and explanation with her, Frappier cut in before they had moved three steps, his full wet lips curled insolently under the hairline mustache, an aura of cologne about him. Duke yielded Jane with reluctance, realizing it was senseless to protest and create a scene.

The next time Duke and Jane tried dancing together, it was Clyde Vorse, the stocky sardonic intellectual, who coldly broke them up within ten feet of their table. And on their third attempt, Gene Desmond was there immediately to claim the girl, recalling their previous meeting outside the Village Barn and smiling with all his volatile charm. Desmond danced with professional skill and grace, holding Jane closer than necessary, and Duke Morey watched with hatred rising and raging inside him, the vision of Desmond and Ann Norvill together seared in his mind.

"Take it easy, Duke," advised Tom Garrick.

"Who you with tonight, Tom?" asked Duke, flat and cold. "Them or me?"

Garrick shook his crisp brown head. "I don't know, Duke. Right in the middle, I guess."

"If you get in my way, you'll get hurt," Duke said.

Garrick smiled wanly. "And if I cross them I'll get killed, Duke."

"You were ready to make a break. Tonight's the time, Tom."

"There's too many of them," Tom Garrick said. "We can't fight them all, Duke. We haven't got a chance."

"You want to go back to Ellinger's and have them beat the truth out of you, about Castelli and Borchek?" demanded Duke Morey. "They will, you know, sooner or later. I wouldn't be surprised if they had a regular torture chamber in that place."

Garrick stared at his glass. "I don't know, Duke, I really don't know."

"Well, you'd better be making up your mind," Duke said. "One way or the other, Tom."

When Duke Morey went to the washroom, hopeful for an opportunity to use a telephone somewhere, Park Lomax drifted along after him, slender, blond, and smiling his nice half-shy boyish smile.

"Why don't you climb on my back, Park, and let me carry you around?" Duke asked, disgustedly.

"It's an idea," Lomax drawled. "But I didn't bring a saddle. I trust you're enjoying yourself, Duke."

"Having the time of my life," Duke assured him. "Why aren't you dancing with my girl?"

"I don't like women," Park Lomax said mildly. "I can't stand their yacking. So far as I'm concerned they're only good for one thing."

"And you've used a lot of 'em for that, haven't you?"

"Not so many. I'm kind of particular and discriminating. Like yourself, Duke ... How much would you give to use a telephone, boy?"

"Ten cents," Duke Morey said promptly. "And I still say a nickle was enough."

Park Lomax laughed softly. "You're a pretty tough boy, Duke. But you aren't tough enough to do what you're planning."

Duke Morey washed his hands slowly and thoughtfully, smiling at Lomax in the mirror. "I haven't got a plan or plot in my head, Park. Can I go back and play with the other kids now, teacher?"

Park Lomax inclined his shapely blond head. "Don't try it, Duke. You aren't that tough. Nobody is."

Walking back to the table, Duke Morey's thoughts were morbid: *They sure got us bottled up tight. Poor little Janie will never know what hit her. I've got to go through with it, and then make my play. That's the only chance, and a damned thin one. If I can't cut it that way, we're both cooked—and very well done, too.*

It was about 10:20, when Jane Tolman left the table to visit the powder room, Duke and Garrick rising with her. Resuming his seat, Duke Morey watched her lithe easy grace, her fine firmly-rounded little figure weaving through the crowd, her dark head and clear lovely chin lifted in a way that made her five-two height seem the equal of any six-foot man.

"It's time, Duke," said Tom Garrick, producing a tiny envelope. "You want me to do it, or will you? Or have you decided not to knock her out?"

"Go ahead, Tom," said Duke dully. "There's no other way. She'll be better off sleeping. You're sure about that stuff, aren't you?"

"Just enough to put her out a couple of hours. It'll take twenty minutes to hit her. It won't hurt her a bit, Duke." With trembling fingers Garrick opened the paper and poured the powder into Jane's fresh drink. Watching him, Duke thought of Ann Norvill and Lolly Durand and Louella Barnes, all the hundreds of others, and he had to fight down the impulse to open up on Garrick right there, blast him and the rest of Ellinger's boys ... But that would not only be suicidal for Jane and himself, it would ruin every prospect of bringing this vice ring to justice.

A few minutes after Jane took the drink, they all left. The company limousine pulled up at the curb and they got into the rear seat with Jane in the middle, while Rudy Valance watched smilingly from his place beside the chauffeur. Less than five minutes later they parked in front of the Fenwick Apartments on Madison Avenue.

"What—what we stopping here for, Duke?" she said.

"Don't worry, you'll be all right, Janie," he said. "I'll take care of you."

They got out, Jane between them, and Rudy Valance whispered: "Dump her and get back here fast, boys, and we'll breeze."

There was nobody in the foyer. They ran the self-operating elevator up to the second floor, and walked into Number 221 without encountering anyone in the gloomy dim-lighted corridor. The apartment was furnished, but empty and unlived in. Jane looked at Duke, puzzlement and passion mixed in her eyes.

Duke looked at Tom instead of Jane. "Tom," he said, "wait outside. I'll be with you in ten minutes."

Garrick stared hard at him. "Ten minutes is all we have, Duke."

"I know," Duke said. "I know." Garrick turned and left, closing the door behind him. Duke was taking a chance on Garrick by doing this, but he figured he could hear if Tom went down the stairs. Besides, no matter what, he had to tell Jane what was happening. In case something went wrong, in case—well, she had to know whose side he was on.

"Janie," he said, as soon as the door closed, "I've got to talk fast. Real fast. I can't give you the whole picture, but you can trust me. I'm here because they're going to try and kidnap you tonight. Ellinger's all one big vice ring, bigger than you or I can imagine. In ten minutes some knockout drops we put in your last drink will put you to sleep. You'll be out two hours. When you wake up—I hope this whole ring will be smashed. Anyway, you'll be safe. I promise you."

Jane looked at Duke, fear in her eyes. "Duke! What are you going to do? You'll be hurt, Duke. You'll be—"

"We don't have much time, Janie. I either have to try and break up this rotten ring, or else throw you—and myself, too—to

Desmond and Frappier and Vorse. I can't tell you anything else. Except that you're not going to be in this room, where they expect to find you. I'm going to take you down the hall somewhere. How do you feel, Janie?"

Duke put his hand on Jane Tolman's waist, slipped it around on her back. She flushed, moved closer instinctively. "Fine, Duke. Better than I've ever felt. Duke?"

"What, Jane!"

"Duke—you said ten minutes. I want you to take me—make love to me—now. Please, Duke. In case one of us, or both of us, don't come out of this horrible thing, I want to have had you. I know—from that first night, Duke, that you want me. At least want me in this way. Want to make love to my body. And more, I think. But no matter what, Duke, make love to me, hard, all over, now."

She started to undress, blouse, skirt coming off quickly, down to her underthings.

"Janie—" Duke started to say.

"I know, Duke. But it won't take that long. Do it, Duke. Take me hard, fast, selfishly, like a man takes a woman purely for his own pleasure. I'll stay with you, Duke. No matter how quickly it happens, it'll happen to me, too. I love you, Duke. If you only knew how badly…Hurry, Duke."

Duke Morey went to Jane, unbuckling his pants with one hand, the other undoing her bra, letting it fall free from her magnificent chest. This was the first time he had really seen her wonderful breasts. They were everything Stella had had, and Ann, and all the women he had ever known. They were magnificent. Rounded but full, perfectly straight from her chest, perfectly white and unmarred, with the most tempting, luscious tips he had ever seen on a woman. "Jane," he said, as he moved his hand against them, feeling the tips grow fuller, harder, longer against his rolling palm, "I love—"

She put her hand over his mouth. "Don't say it, Duke," she whispered. "Don't say it now. Not until this thing is over—if it ever is. Not until you find Ann. But no matter what happens, no matter what you feel, this moment will be all mine. Undress, Duke. No—I'll undress you."

Duke Morey forgot everything then, and for the next few moments, as Jane Tolman, woman personified, bold yet effeminate, breasty yet powerful, confident, lean, undid his pants and shirt, pulled them wildly from his body. He forgot Garrick, standing outside the door, he forgot the men in the car and Ellinger and Ann and everything in the world except for the luscious fantastically driving, pulsating, sexual body making love to him. Duke Morey was all man, he was aggressive, masculine, straight. He had known women who liked to be on top in sex; with Duke they had always ended up on the bottom. He had known women who liked to caress the bodies of men rather than have the men caress their own; but Duke had always ended up doing the feeling. For the first time, all that was different. This five foot two inch, perfectly proportioned piece of virgin female swept over him like a hot hurricane, leaving him standing there in the center of the room, gasping, feeling feelings he'd never felt before, transfixed in passion. He wanted to move, wanted to break away and grab her body and throw it down beneath him and make love to it over and over and to hell with Desmond and Garrick and whoever else would come in and find them there! But he didn't. For sixty seconds, he didn't. He just stood there, as this Woman of women, as this incredibly feminine, aggressive female fell down on the floor at his feet, kissed his ankles with a sexuality that almost exploded him, ran her lips, her hands, her whole body, up his calves, his thighs, torturously to his flat hard stomach, all the time working her opened thighs against him, her hard tipped breasts against him, until each time her nipples touched him he felt like two hard points were actually trying to break into his skin, and each time her thighs fastened around some part of his body he felt their burning moistness as if it were seething lava pouring onto him. And then, just when he felt like it would be all over for him, when he was just a second, a split second away from the clouds and the stars and the sun and the comets, she pulled away from him, stepped back one step and stood, her body twisted in passion, staring at him as no woman had ever stared at a man, her own hands running frantically over her swelled bosom, her thighs squeezing violently together in a semicircle of passion that would have provided enough power to satisfy a thousand men! She was tempting him, teasing him, taunting him, as he had never imagined he could be tempted, taunted, teased. She was standing there, torrid as the inside of the sun, just an arm's length from him, with his own body on the verge of exploding, and she was showing him what she felt! He stood there, unmoving for a split second, transfixed by the infinite heights that they both were reaching now without touching one another, and then, suddenly, she looked at him in a stare of shock, her mouth slacked open, and her hips stopped moving. Her hands stopped moving over her bosom then. Instead she squeezed her breasts hard, until her fists grew white, and her entire body straightened up like a vertical rail in space, on the tips of her toes, her hands streaking like lightning down to her thighs, her nails digging in, drawing blood, at the same time that blood came from her lower lip as her teeth pierced it. She started to moan, deep in her throat, then suddenly, she realized the impossible thing that was happening to her because of her passion for Duke, and she leaped onto him, her arms around his shoulders, her lower limbs on his belly, and they fell to the floor, hard, not caring, as their bodies immediately met, and shuddered. A few seconds later it was all over. A few seconds after that, her mouth slacked once more, her eyes rolled back in her head, and she was asleep.

Duke dressed her quickly, as best he could, then put on his own clothes. He was still shaking from the tremendous thing that had just happened between him, and some of his strength was gone. But, somehow, there was a new kind of power in his limbs.

"What now, Tom?" asked Duke Morey, when he opened the door.

Garrick spread his hands. "That's all for us, Duke. Back to the car and blow." He looked at Duke's appearance, at Jane's, but didn't say anything about it.

"And leave Jane here—for *them?*"

"They won't hurt her, Duke. They won't touch her."

"Desmond would," Duke said. "Frappier and Vorse would. I can't leave her like this, Tom."

"What the hell we going to do?" asked Garrick. "Valance or that chauffeur-gunsel will be up here, if we take too long. Come on, Duke!" He whirled and started for the door.

"Wait a minute, Tom," said Duke Morey, drawing the blunt .38 automatic from his pocket. "Grab the back of your head, boy. I'll take the gun in under your arm."

"What the hell?" Garrick turned, stared in astonishment, and raised his arms to clasp his hands behind his head.

Duke deftly slipped Garrick's pistol from the shoulder-clip, and placed it in his left-hand pocket. "All right, Tom. You can go now."

Garrick shook his head and lowered his arms. "You'll never make it, Duke. You haven't got a chance. They'll be coming any minute."

"Okay, then." Duke motioned toward the bedroom. "Pick her up and carry her out. Get moving, boy! And don't think I won't let you have it, if you try anything."

"Where we taking her, Duke?" Garrick bent over and lifted up the unconscious girl.

Some other apartment," Duke Morey said, prodding Garrick and his dead-weight burden out into the hallway, closing and relocking the door of 221.

They moved along the corridor toward the rear, until they reached an apartment entrance outlined in light. Duke rapped on the door. A plump middle-aged woman opened it, staring aghast at the girl in Garrick's arms. She started to shut the door, but Duke inserted his shoe. The number, he observed, was 233.

"Sorry, lady, it's an emergency. Have you got a phone?"

"Yes, but—"

"We've got to leave this girl here," Duke Morey said. "It may save her life—and ours. Call an ambulance for her, and call the police to Number 221 up the hall. Here's something for your trouble." He pressed a ten-dollar bill into her hand, and pushed the door open so Garrick could carry Jane through and lay her down on the davenport.

"I—I don't know about this business," protested the woman. "She—she ain't dead, is she? I—I don't like this—"

"She'll be all right," Duke said. "All you've got to do is call an ambulance and the cops. An easy way to save a life—and earn ten bucks, isn't it? You won't get into any trouble. I'd call myself, but we've got to get out of here quick."

"You—you don't look like cops to me."

"FBI," Duke said. "Please do what I told you and thanks a lot. Is there a back way out of here?" She nodded and pointed toward the rear of the building, and Duke said, "Thanks again, lady. Come on, Tom."

They went out and heard the door hastily locked behind them. At the end of the corridor they found a dark dingy back stairway, and Tom Garrick hesitated. "They may be covering out back, Duke."

"We'll risk it," Duke said. "You make a good shield."

Garrick started down the stairs. "You really going to fight the whole outfit?"

"That's right, Tom."

"What the hell are you? A cop—or just crazy?"

"Maybe both," Duke Morey said, grinning. "Keep moving."

Tom Garrick halted and turned. "Give me my gun, Duke. I'll fight them with you."

"Who's crazy now?"

"I mean it, Duke. Honest to God," Garrick said, choked and earnest. "I'd like nothing better than to break that filthy bunch of bastards!"

"We'll see, Tom," said Duke. "I've got to be real sure. And I've got to get somewhere to phone from. Didn't dare wait upstairs."

"I'm with you, Duke. I'll prove it, if I get a chance."

"I'm not the law. I'm all alone in this, Tom."

Tom Garrick gestured. "I don't care a damn what you are, Duke! I'm on your side—all the way."

They descended all the way into the basement, and went up some chipped stone steps and out through an opened bulkhead door, into the odorous darkness of a backyard lined with garbage barrels and ashcans, littered with tin cans and broken bottles and refuse of all kinds. With Garrick in the lead, they picked their way across the lot, Duke Morey holding the stubby .38 in his right-hand pocket

The form of Rudy Valance loomed suddenly before them in the shadows, a leveled automatic glinting in his steady right hand.

CHAPTER SIXTEEN

"What's going on here?" inquired Rudy Valance, dark face smiling with suave mockery under the white Panama hat. "What kind of a game you boys trying to play?"

"Look, Rudy, I'll show you," Tom Garrick said, quickly and easily, holding out his closed left hand and opening it slowly, palm upward.

Rudy Valance peered down at it in the vague light. Garrick brought his right fist whipping up in a wicked uppercut to the chin. Valance's sleek head snapped far back, the white hat sailing off it, and his arms jerked upward as his knees started folding. The pistol exploded on a high bright slant, and a window pane shattered in the background. Rudy Valance was falling in slow-motion, when Duke Morey stepped forward and slashed down with his gun barrel. Valance groaned and dropped flat on his face, the automatic rolling clear as he slacked into a motionless hulk in the ash-grayed dirt and rubble.

"Can I have this, Duke?" pleaded Garrick, picking up the gun.

"All right, keep it," Duke said. "But don't try to turn it on me."

"Aren't you sure yet?"

"Not entirely."

Someone was running down the narrow cluttered passage from the street, coming in their direction, and they whirled with guns poised. "Rudy?" a voice called, hoarse and panting, and light slanting from a lower window rayed across Ellinger's liveried chauffeur, pistol in hand. Duke and Garrick fired almost simultaneously, their guns blaring into the alley with a tremendous roar. The chauffer lurched into one wall, blundered across against the other side, upset a rubbish barrel and toppled headlong across it, coming to rest at last in a flood of debris spilling from the rusty castiron container.

"Sure now?" asked Tom Garrick, grinning wildly.

"Pretty sure," Duke Morey said. "Let's move out of here."

They fled along the rear of buildings, stumbling over cans and ashpiles, slipping on bottles, and turned through another vile black alley. Angling off again into a back area, they scaled an old board fence and crossed a weedgrown open lot surrounded by huge advertising signs. Creeping out from beneath arc-lighted billboards, they followed side streets and alley ways until they emerged on a bright busy thoroughfare and spotted a corner drugstore.

"I've got to phone," Duke said, limping in agony now on his bad leg.

"It won't do much good to call the cops," protested Garrick.

"I'll call the FBI too. Is that good enough?"

"You *are* FBI then?"

"No, I'm just a citizen," Duke Morey said, "Just an ex-GI."

Garrick wiped his sweaty face with a linen handkerchief. "Even the FBI won't get to Ellinger right away. He must have a dozen secret passages out of that building, Duke."

"*We* might get to him, Tom," said Duke, spitting cotton from his dry mouth. "If we get back there before the alarm's out, we might get to Ellinger and Zolnay and Kern." He bent to massage that left leg.

Garrick shook his head. "They'll know we're on the loose before we ever get back there, Duke. They probably know it right now."

"I suppose so. If the follow-up men reached the Fenwick."

In the crowded drugstore the telephone booth was occupied, and they waited with nervous impatience for the woman to cease babbling into the mouthpiece. The harder they looked at her, the more intent she was on talking all night. "There ought to be a law," Garrick muttered, amber eyes flicking from one entrance to the other.

"When I get in there—if ever," Duke Morey said. "Stay where I can see you, Tom, and watch the doors."

"Sure, I'll keep on the lookout, Duke," said Garrick. "But you don't have to watch me, boy. I'm in it for the duration now. Maybe it'll take some of that taste out of my mouth."

Finally the woman hung up and came out, high-headed and smirking, and Duke Morey slid into the small hot booth that reeked of cheap perfume. He called the Twenty-fifth Precinct and told them of the change in plans, directing them to the Fenwick on Madison, Numbers 221 and 233. He also advised the police to throw a cordon around Ellinger's brownstone building, and to call in the FBI if they deemed it essential, since kidnapping was one of the crimes involved … Duke was sweating all over and half-suffocated before he finished, ill from the cloying scent of the last occupant.

The sergeant on the desk didn't seem inclined to take Duke too seriously either. He had probably seen too many of these big life-and-death cases turn into meaningless fiascoes. But Duke did the best he could on the wire. It was a relief to get out of those smothering confines, and breathe even drugstore air stirred by electric fans.

Tom Garrick was waiting, tall and alert under his air of nonchalance, gunhand in his coat pocket. Passing girls turned for a second glance to those two big clean-cut young men in their flaw-lessly tailored suits, but Garrick and Duke Morey had deeper darker things in mind this night. They were flirting with death, rather than with soft fragrant pretty girls. Heedless of the warm feminine eyes, they stood in thoughtful meditation and quiet debate.

"Let's take a chance, Tom," said Duke. "Grab a taxi to Ellinger's and go after the big ones."

"Might as well," conceded Garrick. "Can't get in any deeper than we are, Duke."

Feeling the pressure of time and danger, afraid for Jane Tolman, although she should be safe, Duke Morey led the way out of the drugstore and looked around for a cab. If the follow-up crew had been slow in arriving at the Fenwick Apartments, there was still a chance for Duke and Tom to get to Ellinger's before their dereliction was noted and reported to headquarters. Easier and quicker and surer than any law force, with free access to the brownstone building, they might be able to get Ellinger and Kern and Zolnay under their guns. With luck, and lots of it.

But their luck ran out right then and there, as Clyde Vorse and Payton Frappier appeared with dramatic and startling suddenness, and stood eyeing them with cold hostile curiosity.

"You boys should be home in bed by now," Frappier said, idly fingering his narrow mustache. "You completed your mission. Why aren't you following the normal procedure?"

"What were you doing in that phone booth, Morey?" demanded Vorse, his mouth thin and cruel under the arrogant nose.

"Looking for dimes in the return slot."

"Don't hand me any of your sophomoric wit," Vorse said harshly. "Give me a straight answer, Morey. Who were you phoning?"

"Nobody that concerns you, Vorse," said Duke, thinking: They're suspicious, but they don't know what's happened yet.

"You're on the spot, Morey. Anything you do concerns us."

Tom Garrick said lightly: "Can't a guy call a girl, if he wants to, Clyde? The Duke just had to ditch a nice little brunette, you know."

"Nobody's questioning *you*—yet," Clyde Vorse said. "He wasn't calling any girl. Where's Valance and the limousine? Gone the way Castelli and Borchek went? What are you trying to pull here anyway?"

"Who the hell made you commander-in-chief?" Tom Garrick asked angrily. "Go on about your own business, Vorse."

"Not a chance," Vorse said, taut-lipped and bleak. "You're coming with us. We're taking you back to Ellinger's."

"That's the ticket, Clyde," approved Payton Frappier. "If they were on the level, they wouldn't be running around loose tonight. They'd be home, or on their way home in that town car. You'd better come quietly, gentlemen."

"Come on, come on," Vorse said impatiently, right hand dipping into his coat pocket.

Duke Morey was lounging at ease, hands in jacket pockets, the .38 warming in the grip of his right palm. "I don't think so," he said quietly. "Even you can be wrong, Vorse."

Surprisingly, it was little Payton Frappier who made the first outright move, his manicured hand darting under the long rolled lapel on his double-breasted coat, but Tom Garrick clipped him squarely on the jaw, driving him clear across the sidewalk into a Nedick soft-drink counter. People scattered and women screamed, as Frappier bounced off the bar and fell on his knees, marcelled head drooping and blood running from his flabby mouth.

Clyde Vorse's hand was working busily in his pocket, but Duke Morey tilted up the blunt automatic in his own pocket and fired swiftly through the flannel cloth. Flame stabbed out and lashed Vorse into a backward stagger against the corner lamp post. Vorse's wild shot smashed the plateglass of the drugstore window into ragged jangling shards and splinters, cascading with brittle music onto the concrete. Duke Morey, his gun clear this time, blasted Vorse again, ripping him loose from the post. Doubled over and crawling at his abdomen, Clyde Vorse writhed down into the gutter, stiffened out spasmodically, and went limp, loose and lifeless against the curb.

Payton Frappier had heaved himself upright and hauled his pistol out, but Tom Garrick was leveled off and shooting before

Frappier could trigger, the fire spurting loudly, the bullets rocking Frappier back against the Nedick stand once more. He flopped forward in a disjointed sprawl, sleek mustached face scraping the cement walk, and a large glass bowl of orange pop crashed down beside him, showering Frappier's dapper body with liquid and sparkling fragments.

People were fleeing frantically in all directions, women shrieking hysterically and men shouting hoarsely, and police whistles shrilled somewhere. In the street automobile horns trumpeted, brakes screeched and tires squealed on the pavement, and steel bumpers clashed and clanged in a sudden jam of traffic.

Duke Morey and Tom Garrick, guns still swinging in their hands, raced along the walk looking for a taxi to commandeer, and everybody was giving them plenty of room, dodging and running in panic before them. They could both move fast, and nobody tried to stop them. A block away from the scene, they turned into a dim quiet side street, and were loping along there when a shining silver-colored convertible swerved in to the curb beside them.

Duke saw the coppery-red sheen of Stella Leeds' head, as she leaned out and beckoned them into the car. Breathless, sobbing for air, they plunged into the rear seat, and Stella whipped the powerful machine away with a reckless but expert hand, slowing to cruise at a normal rate once they were well away, with no signs of pursuit behind them. Duke Morey lay back on the rich leather, welcoming the rush of night air on his sweaty head and face, setting his teeth against the grinding pain in his wounded left leg, that was making him faint and giddy.

"Almost forgot about that leg," he groaned. "It's sure giving me hell now."

"You can still run all right, Duke," said Garrick.

"Have to be scared now," Duke said, smiling. "You should've seen me in my prime, son. The Wisconsin Whippet, they used to call me."

Garrick laughed. "I was known as the Stanford Streak myself. Fastest thing on the Coast, kid."

Duke Morey grinned wryly. "Well, we've both come a long ways, Tom."

"Yeah, a long ways down," Tom Garrick said.

Stella Leeds, slowing down still more, motioned for them to climb over into the front seat. Duke said: "Go ahead, Tom. My leg hurts too much." Garrick clambered over to sit beside Stella, and she signaled again for Duke. Grumbling, he moved forward and lowered himself carefully into the leather between them, the remembered perfume of Stella in his nostrils.

"Couldn't talk with you back there," she explained. "You boys seem to be in a bit of trouble."

"Where you going?" Duke asked.

"Why, you want to go to Ellinger's, don't you?"

"Sure, we do."

"I shouldn't think you would, Duke."

"You saw what happened on that corner?"

"I got a glimpse of the fireworks." Stella Leeds laughed her cool lilting laugh. "Mutiny in the ranks. What's this revolution all about anyway?"

Duke Morey scanned her pure profile. "You don't know, Stella?"

"How would I know, Duke?"

"You don't miss anything that goes on at Ellinger's," he told her.

Stella laughed again. "Perhaps not—once. But I've lost contact, of late. I knew something like this was coming though. I could see it the minute I first looked at you, Duke."

"Smart girl."

"I told you there'd come a time when you needed help—from me," Stella Leeds reminded him.

"How can you help us?" asked Duke Morey.

"I can hide you out—in my apartment. The police will be after you, along with Ellinger's gang. You're too hot to circulate around this town."

"Somebody might have spotted this car, or got your license number."

Stella shook her auburn head. "Nobody around when I picked you up."

"Always someone around," Garrick put in. "You better drop us somewhere."

"We can at least have a drink in my place," she said.

"No," Duke said curtly. "We haven't got time to fool around. Take us to Ellinger's."

"Just like that?" mocked Stella Leeds. "I happen to know your birds have flown, boys. You won't find Ellinger or Zolnay or Kern at headquarters."

"You must be equipped with radar," Tom Garrick remarked.

"Where've they gone?" inquired Duke, skeptically.

"I *might* tell you," Stella said, teasingly. "I might even take you there. If you're real nice and agreeable to me."

"What would that entail? A toss in the hay?" Garrick said, with satire.

Stella Leeds was unperturbed. "Could be. Some such thing. Interested, gentlemen?"

"Not much," Garrick said.

"Not at all," Duke Morey said. "We've got things to do tonight."

"You want to find the Big Three, don't you? You never will without me. I can take you right to them."

Tom Garrick laughed mirthlessly. "You'll take us all right! To the furnace or the lye vat, or whatever it is Horace Ellinger uses."

Stella looked scornfully at them. "You damned fools! I'm trying to help you. Did it ever occur to you that I could have some excellent personal reasons for wishing the worst to Horace and his hatchet men? That I might want to get in on the right side—at this late date?"

"You really know where they are tonight, Stella?" asked Duke.

She nodded firmly. "I do, Duke. And I'll drive you there—when the time's right. Meanwhile we're stopping at my apartment for a drink."

Duke and Garrick exchanged dubious puzzled glances, and Stella Leeds went on: "I'm fairly sick of this show myself. I've taken a lot from Ellinger and his whole fouled-up crew. I'm ready to hit back."

"All right, Stella," said Duke wearily, shifting his aching leg. "We'll stop at your place, Anything you say ... As long as you take us to Ellinger and the others—in time."

"Too early to go out there now," Stella Leeds said. "Ellinger and his staff are in conference with some out-of-town agents. It's better to wait until the others leave."

"By then they'll know what happened and be gunning for us," Garrick protested.

"Maybe not—if our luck holds," said Stella. "Ellinger doesn't often accept messages when he's in conference at the Chateau."

CHAPTER SEVENTEEN

The apartment was as Duke Morey remembered it, luxurious and comfortable and ultra-smart, gleaming with a soft rich patina under the mellow golden light. He observed that Tom Garrick was quite at home there, and reflected bitterly that Desmond and Lomax and all the rest would have been likewise. Garrick selected a long thin cigar from a hammered-silver box, stretching back at ease, and Duke surveyed the book shelves again, marveling how such an intelligent woman could be so unmoral or ammoral. There were still more of his favorite authors: Robert Penn Warren, Michael Foster, Herge-sheimer, Arlen, Fowler, Wakeman, Busch, Wylie, Benet, Ford Madox Ford, Jackson, Burnett, Merle Miller, Schulberg, and Irwin Shaw. A library that he'd like to own himself.

Stella Leeds brought them drinks, tall and smooth and strong, the ice clinking in the thin glasses, and they relaxed a little and drank with pleasure. After preparing a second round, Stella said: "Tom, I want to talk privately with Duke. You don't mind, do you?"

Garrick grinned. "Not at all. I'll just settle down with a good book."

Vaguely embarrassed and troubled, Duke Morey followed Stella into the familiar elegance of that bedroom, limping slightly on his left leg, and watched her close the door. She seated herself on the edge of the bed and patted the spot beside her, but Duke sat down in a chair facing her at a fairly safe distance. Looking at the breath-taking lines of her face and throat, her breasts and hips and legs, Duke knew that, whatever she was, Stella Leeds still had a powerful appeal for him. But he had no intention of yielding to it, tonight or ever again.

"Duke, I'm going to be frank," she said. "And it'll no doubt shock you. But I want you, Duke, I have ever since—that one night. I've been burning for you, and there's nobody else. Just thinking of you, darling, sets me on fire. Is it—is it too much to ask?"

"I'm afraid it is, Stella."

"You're in love with that Jane Tolman?"

"I don't know," Duke Morey said slowly. "I was in love with a girl, but she disappeared—while I was in Korea."

"Ann Norvill?"

"You know all about that, too?"

Stella Leeds inclined her head, burnished to red-gold in the lamplight. "Yes, I know," she faltered, and then her head came up and the strange green eyes fixed on him. "Duke, I'll get her out of—that place. I'll do anything for you."

"Too late for that," he said. "She wouldn't want to leave. She doesn't want to see me—or anyone she used to know. She's ruined, Stella, worse than dead."

"Oh, Duke, darling," she sighed. "Look at me, Duke. Come to me. Take me in your arms, darling. Please hold me and kiss me—just this once."

He shook his crewcut head, studied the glass in his hand, and drank deeply. "There's no use, Stella. It's no good."

"You wish it hadn't happened before, don't you?"

Duke raised his wide shoulders a trifle. "I thought I had something rare and wonderful—until I got back to Ellinger's that noon."

"Those bastards!"

"What can you expect?"

"Nothing, I know—nothing at all." Stella Leeds gulped her drink down, almost desperately, rising and setting the glass on her dressing table and swaying toward him, her fragrant near-ness rioting in his senses. Duke stood up quickly, still holding his drink. "Take me, Duke, please take me," she cried, half-sobbing, her eyes and face tortured, coming against him with thrusting breasts and loins and frenzied clinging arms. Revolted, yet sorry for her, he backed awkwardly away, and still she gripped and grappled at him, in blind shameless fury and lust.

"Goddamn it, Stella," he muttered, in exasperation, handi-capped with the glass in his hand, feeling ridiculous and ashamed for her wantonness.

"All right!" She let go of him and swung savagely, knocking the drink out of his hand and slapping him hard on the cheek. Catching her wrists then, amazed at the wiry explosive strength of the girl, Duke Morey held her off, forced her back, and flung her across the bed. Stella lay there sobbing heartbrokenly, her classic features buried in the satin spread, her coppery hair fired by the lamplight.

After watching her helplessly for a minute, Duke turned and left the bedroom, disregarding Garrick's saturnine smile, limp-ing to the bar to mix himself another highball.

Solemn again, Tom Garrick came and stood beside him. "What's the matter, Duke?"

"She's crazy."

"Nymphomania," mused Garrick. "An awful thing... Will she take us to them?"

"I don't know, Tom. Who can tell what she'll do?"

"Is it worth the chance, Duke?"

"For me, it is," Duke Morey said simply.

"I'll string along then," Garrick said. "I know about where the Chateau is, I think. If we left it to the law, Ellinger would get out of it some way. Ellinger and all his key men."

Duke nodded. "They've got to die, Tom."

"Well, we've made a pretty good start on them, Duke," said Tom Garrick, pouring scotch into his glass...

When Stella Leeds came out of the bedroom a few minutes later, she was perfectly calm and composed, serene and cool, queenlike in her poised beauty. "I guess we can start now, anytime you boys are ready. But there's no hurry. We might as well have one more for the road."

Outside in the silver convertible, with Garrick in the center and Duke Morey on the outer edge this time, Stella Leeds drove with speed and assurance, the night breeze whipping their heads and faces. A yellow moon soared above the lofty shafts and towers of Manhattan, and the sky was dusted brilliantly with farflung stars. They rode out past the unreal summer greenery of Central Park, through the garish populous stretches of Harlem and into the Bronx, with Yankee Stadium and the Polo Grounds looming against the luminous night heavens. Riding in silence, for the most part, heading for Ellinger's suburban hideout.

Duke felt nothing but pity for Stella Leeds now, sorrow for a twisted life that might have been beautiful and worthwhile. Everybody has something riding and driving them through this world, he thought. Stella and her insatiable desire, her obsession with sex. With Lolly Durand it had been curiosity, a naive longing to be a sophisticated woman of the world. Tom Garrick's burden was one of shame and guilt, for the kind of life he'd been living at Ellinger's Escort Service. Horace Ellinger himself, as well as Kern and Zolnay, was goaded by greed for more power and more wealth.

Gene Desmond was like a male Stella Leeds, in endless quest of sexual pleasure and fleshly delights. Park Lomax, Duke couldn't figure out ... Payton Frappier had been on the borderline of perversion, yet he had fought and died gamely in that street-corner gunfight. Clyde Vorse evidently had patterned himself after the Nazis or Reds, supremely contemptuous of humanity in general, scornful of life and love and death.

Duke didn't know exactly what harassed Jane Tolman, unless it was loneliness and aimlessness. She should have been married.

Her poetry and advertising work were not enough for a woman like Jane, who was meant to be a wife and mother ... As for Duke Morey himself, he had been hounded by the need of finding Ann Norvill. Now that was dead and gone, and there wasn't much left. Nothing but hate and fury, the bloodlust to avenge himself on Desmond and Lomax, Ellinger and Zolnay and Kern.

"Horace Ellinger will beat almost any rap they bring against him," Stella Leeds said abruptly. "He has done it before, by sacrificing a few stooges and underlings. He has been in the rackets, a vice lord all his life, and not a single smirch on his record. Ellinger's power reaches beyond City Hall and the Legislature at Albany, to the cities all over the country. It's uncanny, incredible ..."

Stella Leeds laughed, a low musical sound that rippled with gentle mockery of all mankind and everything in the universe. "Nothing but bullets will stop Ellinger and his men. That's why I'm taking you to the Chateau tonight. I want them dead."

They must have hurt this girl terribly, Duke Morey thought, along with all the other women they have destroyed. Probably they broke her in and started her off, made her life what it is now, a blind burning progression from one pair of masculine arms to another.

"Can we get into the Chateau, Stella?" asked Tom Garrick.

"With me, you can," she said. "Alone you wouldn't get to first base."

Duke Morey tried to recall what he had heard about this place known as the Chateau, a grand walled-in mansion on the rocky heights overlooking the Hudson River, where the topflight hoodlums and racketeers of the nation sometimes convened. Scraps of gossip had reached Duke's ears about unbelievable orgies held there, mass executions and purges, a medieval torture chamber, and a secret underground tomb. Things that seemed impossible in this modern age, but which existed beyond any reasonable doubt. An organization, backed by unlimited funds, strong enough to defy all the law and order in the United States, because money-hungry politicians on all levels could be bought and sold, owned and enslaved completely.

Duke glanced past Garrick to the keen profile and wind-blown coppery hair of Stella Leeds. In spite of his revulsion, he had wanted her and been tempted back there in her bedroom, and he hated himself for that weakness and need. Duke Morey tried to rationalize his feelings about the opposite sex. *"What have you got against women?"* Gene Desmond had asked him...He *did* have something against them, Duke realized, with some surprise. He didn't really *like* women, and never had. He couldn't stand their chatter any more than Park Lomax could. Duke actually resented them, because he recognized their physical desirability and necessity. It was irksome to have to require and rely on such inferior creatures, most of whom hadn't a thought in the world beyond clothes, cosmetics, hairdos, jewels, parties, and men.

There were exceptions, of course. Ann Norvill was an exception, or had been. In her own peculiar way Stella Leeds belonged in this sparse selective category, and Jane Tolman—she was unique. God—what incredible sexuality! But women by and large were nothing, no good, simple and shallow, vain and stupid, brainless instruments of sex and propogation. Duke Morey was rather shocked at this sudden summary. He had never thought of himself as a woman-hater, but there it was. He hated them because he needed them. They were a prime requisite to a man's full well-rounded life, and in general they were far from worthy. Governed by emotion rather than intelligence, dominated and driven by sex instead of sense, acting on weird unreasonable impulses, straws in the wind.

Women, he thought, with contempt and abhorrence. The cross men have to bear is their dependence on females. Observe the conduct of women, brawling ruthlessly at bargain counters, hogging the road when they drive cars and the sidewalk when on foot, always pushing and crowding ahead in any waiting line, absolutely devoid of consideration, sympathy and respect.

Conceited, egocentric, selfish, and arrogant, as false as their artificial eyelashes and inflated rubber bosoms and tight-girdled waists, their makeup masked faces and lipsticked mouths and bottled fragrance. Exhibitionists, given to all kinds of provocative and indecent exposures ... He recalled circuses he had seen in certain bagnios. White women coupled with giant Negroes and various animals and one another, before paying audiences. There's nothing too low for them, he thought, no depths to which they will not sink and wallow.

To hell with them all, Duke Morey thought, with acid bitterness. Now that Ann Norvill was gone from him, he was through with women. Jane Tolman was one in a million, but was he good enough for her? Maybe he'd just take them as he needed them, the way a man takes a needed drink, but he wouldn't become entangled with them. Not ever again. Unless—he couldn't forget Jane. Even now as he thought of her, his desire grew, his body ached.

The city was behind them now, its glare flung high into the night sky, and the suburbs were dropping away, as the silver convertible sped smoothly along the highway into the north.

CHAPTER EIGHTEEN

A dim face appeared behind the grilled iron gate in the great brick wall, as Stella Leeds stopped the car and blew the horn before it, and the gate opened when the girl and the machine were identified. There were two men on guard, stone-faced and cold-eyed, and one of them said, "Wasn't expectin' you tonight, Miss Leeds," as the car rolled through. "Something came up in town," Stella told him, and stepped on the accelerator, climbing the long winding driveway toward the darkened gloomy pile of the massive stone house on the summit.

The place looked deserted and there was no automobiles in the yard, when Stella drove around back and cut the motor, but she said: "They're here. The cars are in the garage." They got out, stretching and yawning nervously, and Duke Morey felt a cool fresh breeze from the Hudson. Stella led them toward the rear of the main building, where light issued faintly from the basement, and down a short wide flight of outside stairs to an iron-bound oaken door. Duke and Garrick waited, tension taut and aching inside them, while Stella located and rang a hidden bell. They were holding the guns in their pockets, and Duke's palm was damp with sweat on the grip.

A tiny shutter slid open in the door, revealing the seamed homely face of Spider Pratt, the handyman. "What you want here, lady?" he asked, eyes squinting into the outer darkness.

"We're here to report, Spider," she said. "Don't be coy with me."

"They didn't tell me you was comin', Miss Leeds."

"There are lots of things they don't tell you. Open up, Spider."

"They've gone back," Spider Pratt said. "Bad news from the city, I think."

"Somebody's still here," she insisted. "Open the doors."

"I don't know. I'm pretty sure they all went."

"Well, let us in to get a drink, at least," Stella Leeds ordered brusquely. "What's the matter with you tonight, Spider?"

"Something's gone wrong, awful wrong," Spider Pratt mumbled. "They didn't tell me nothin', but I can feel it."

The door opened into a large paneled lounge, fitted in leather and chrome, with a bar on the right side and a staircase rising at the far end. Duke and Garrick scanned the interior and listened intently, but there was nothing to be seen or heard.

"I think you're keeping a woman out here, Spider," said Stella.

Pratt grinned, showing tobacco-stained teeth. "You know better'n that. Them days are gone forever—for me." He moved over behind the bar. "Evenin', Mr. Tom, Mr. Duke. What you folks drinkin' tonight?"

They ordered and Spider busied himself with bottles and glasses and ice, never happier than when mixing drinks and waiting on people.

"Who's left here?" asked Stella.

"Nobody I know of. A call come in and they all took off for town." But he seemed nervous and apprehensive again, his pouched eyes flickering toward the stairway, his hands fumbling the glassware.

"You're lying, Spider."

"I ain't lyin'. Why should I lie? I'm just kinda keyed up tonight. Somethin' bad musta broke in the city. Mr. Ellinger and Mr. Kern and Mr. Zolnay, they all looked plenty worried and mad."

"Who else was here?"

"Big wheels from all over. I don't know them by name. They don't pay no attention to me, Miss Stella. All I do is mix 'em drinks and pass 'em cigars and sandwiches and stuff. That Mr. Ellinger, he never touches liquor or tobacco or nothin', he's a great man."

Duke Morey smiled and nodded. "That he is, Spider."

"A clean-livin' man," Spider Pratt said. "There ain't many like him today. A good man to work for. He always used me good."

"You been with him a long time, Spider?" asked Duke.

"Ever since I was a snotnose kid—beggin' your pardon, ma'am. Here's your drinks, folks. You won't get no better at the Waldorf."

"You're a talented bartender, Spider," said Tom Garrick.

"I'm handy," Spider Pratt admitted modestly. "Mr. Ellinger always said I was awful handy."

They lighted cigarettes and sipped their drinks, and Spider blinked and beamed at them from behind the bar. Duke Morey was wondering what to do next. Apparently Ellinger and his men had received word about their activities in town. The disappearance of Jane Tolman from Number 221 in the Fenwick, the gunwhipping of Rudy Valance and the shooting of the chauffeur, the killing of Clyde Vorse and Payton Frappier. They'd never get to Ellinger at headquarters now. They'd have to turn the case over to the police and the FBI. Perhaps the cops had nabbed some of Ellinger's operatives in that apartment house on Madison. There might be a few convictions for the kidnapping attempt on Jane, but Ellinger and Zolnay and Kern would go free. So would Desmond and Lomax... While Duke and Garrick would have to face charges of murder or manslaughter. It didn't look good at all.

Duke Morey saw the sudden change in Spider Pratt's eyes and wizened features, and he turned away from the bar and saw Park Lomax slouching lazily on the stairway, left hand on the banister, a big blue automatic in his right. Lomax looked blond and boyish and lanquid, an almost apologetic smile on his lean face, as he drawled: "Keep your hands out of your pockets, boys.

Empty and open, where I can see 'em. Duke, you didn't take my advice ... Stella, you're traveling in pretty fast company tonight."

Rapid footsteps sounded from above him, as Duke and his two companions stood frozen and helpless before the bar, and Gene Desmond descended into view, large and handsome, wavy black hair agleam, eyes bluer than ever. He passed Lomax with a light slap on the shoulder, left him there midway on the staircase, and moved across the floor with easy grace and assurance, careful to stay out of Lomax's field of fire.

"Well, Stella, this is a nice bundle you're delivering," Gene Desmond said. "I figured you'd come through, but Horace and the others were a bit worried. Thought maybe you'd fallen for the Duke here, and would try to cover him up."

Stella Leeds glanced quickly at Duke, as if to deny the double-cross intention, but Duke Morey was watching Desmond and Lomax and estimating his chances, oblivious to the girl. "Sure, I always produce, don't I, Gene?" said Stella Leeds, putting down her glass and placing a fresh cigarette in her mouth. "Must be the early training you gave me."

Desmond circled in back of them, and said: "Reach up high, boys. I'll take your guns, and we'll call Horace and the boys back out here. He's going to be very glad to see you two fellahs. It annoys Horace to have some of his key men rubbed out, and he has a special treatment reserved for double-dealers like you. Now don't act up any, because my boy Lomax shoots straight and fast." He stepped up from behind to frisk them with practiced speed and efficiency. Stella Leeds, fumbling in her bag for matches or a lighter, had drifted out toward midfloor.

Desmond had Duke's .38 and was reaching into the left-hand pocket for the .45 Duke had taken from Garrick, when a gun crashed in the center of the room. Stella Leeds had pulled a small snub-nosed pistol from her purse, and fired swiftly at Lomax on the stairway. Park Lomax doubled forward, mild surprise in his bleached eyes and shocked face. Drooping across the banister, blond head hanging, Lomax slid to the bottom and stuck there, wedged against the newel post, his Luger exploding one involuntary shot into the parquet floor.

Stella was swerving her weapon to bear on Desmond, but Gene spun and slashed two slugs from the .38 into her lithe body, jolting her back across the room and against the paneled wall. The pistol dropped from her hand, and Stella Leeds hung there clutching at her breasts, green eyes wide with horror.

Before Gene Desmond could turn back again, Tom Garrick slugged him behind the ear with crushing force, springing the curly black head and driving him forward. Desmond was leaning and tottering, when Duke Morey drew and struck savagely with the .45 Colt, beating him face downward. Duke wheeled on Pratt, but Spider was already shaking his head and reaching for the ceiling, in a frenzy of fear.

Tom Garrick stalked toward the stairway, Valance's gun in his hand now, and Park Lomax was struggling on the rail, straining to push himself erect and lift the Luger. The automatic flamed into the floor in front of Garrick, and Tom lined his pistol and let go at the crumpled figure. The bullet lifted Lomax backward off the banister, and flung him into the wall, where he dropped and rolled loosely to the bottom of the steps. Garrick went to him and picked up the Luger and stood watching the head of the stairs.

Stella Leeds, still propped against the wall with crimson hands gripping her bosom, cried out in weak warning, as Gene Desmond twisted about on the floor and raised the .38 toward Duke Morey. Duke whirled, the muzzle blast leaping upward and scorching his eyeballs, and threw down on Desmond, the big .45 flaring and jerking in his right hand. Teeth bared and eyes slitted to gray-green fire, Duke Morey hammered shots into Gene Desmond's shuddering body, until it was a shattered hulk in a dark spreading pool on the parquet surface.

Duke turned to Pratt, the smoking gun in his hand. "Anybody else upstairs, Spider?"

"No, no, I don't think so, Mr. Duke. So help me. I didn't know them two was here. Honest to God, I didn't know it!"

Garrick spoke from the foot of the staircase. "If there were any more up there they'd be moving in before now, Duke."

"Better watch it a little longer though, Tom." Duke Morey walked across the floor, just in time to catch Stella Leeds as she collapsed, and ease her down onto the leather lounge there. "We'll get you to a doctor, Stella."

She shook her copper-red head slowly and tried to smile. "No good, Duke," panted Stella Leeds. "I've had it—I've got mine, darling. But you see—I was on the right side—on your side—at the end."

"Yes, Stella," he said gently. "You got us out of that one all right."

"Too bad, Duke," murmured Stella Leeds. "We met—too late." Her green eyes lighted and distended with agony, blurred and dulled into blankness. Her red-gold head dropped, a spasm shook her, and then she was still and dead.

Duke Morey turned away from her. "Let's get out of here, Tom. Come on, Spider, you're going along with us."

"I can't, I can't go!" wailed Pratt. "I got orders to stay here, Mr. Duke. Mr. Ellinger told me—"

"To hell with Mr. Ellinger," said Duke. "You're riding out with us, Spider. We may be able to use you in town."

Tom Garrick paused in midroom and stared somberly at the body of the girl. "I can't figure that Stella. Which side was she on anyway?"

"She did some switching, I guess," Duke Morey said. "But she sure wound up on the right team, Tom."

"Which was a damn good thing for us," Garrick said, with a sober grin. "They had us cold, Duke. We were a couple of pigeons."

"You want your gun back? It's not much good unless you've got some more forty-fives."

"Keep it, Duke. Here's another clip for it." Garrick handed it over, and Duke put the new clip in the Colt. "I kind of like this Luger, and Park had a fresh clip in his pocket ... But how we going to get to the big ones now?"

"I don't know—yet," Duke Morey said.

"We'll never get into that brownstone building again. The whole outfit's gunning for us by this time."

"Maybe, with Spider's kind assistance," Duke mused, "we can get them to come to us tonight. Let's go, Spider."

"You boys ain't got a chance," Spider Pratt said, wagging his narrow head. "You won't even get out through the gate down there."

Tom Garrick reached across the bar with a long arm, and grabbed a bottle of White Horse and one of bonded bourbon. "This might come in handy, too."

At the door, Duke Morey glanced back over his shoulder. Stella Leeds lay on the leather divan at the left, with Gene Desmond huddled in midfloor, and Park Lomax stretched at the bottom of the stairway, blond head reflecting the light. They went out and climbed the stone steps into the backyard, eyes ranging the darkness and guns ready in hand. "You drive, Tom," said Duke, prodding Spider into the middle of the front seat and climbing in beside him.

Stella had left the key in the ignition. Garrick started the motor and swung the long low convertible around, hitting the driveway and looping downhill toward the gate in the high brick wall, the Luger in his lap. Duke Morey held the Colt in his hand, the .38 he had retrieved from Desmond in his coat pocket. They might have to shoot their way out.

But they didn't. The guards recognized the silver car and opened the iron gate, and Tom Garrick stepped on the gas and hurled the powerful machine through it and onto the highway, turning back toward the lights of New York.

Spider Pratt shivered on the seat between them. "I don't like this, ridin' in a dead woman's car."

"Death is rampant tonight, Spider," said Duke Morey, smiling thinly into the wind. The men who had contributed most to the destruction of Ann Norvill had paid with their lives now: Desmond and Lomax, Vorse and Frappier, Castelli and Borchek...But the ones really responsible for it, the Big Three, were still living and unharmed, a cancerous menace at the heart of Manhattan.

A plan was evolving in Duke's mind, as they skimmed smoothly through the night. It might not work, but it was well worth trying. Anything to get Horace Ellinger and Rufus Kern and Ben Zolnay, wipe out their evil organization once and for all.

Then Duke Morey was going across the river and find a house at 1260 Brushwood in a certain town, and take Ann Norvill out of that house, willingly or not. She could still be rehabilitated and restored, he thought. It wasn't too late. A girl like Ann was always worth saving, even if she had passed beyond believing it herself.

CHAPTER NINETEEN

In the outer reaches of the city, a great orange-and-blue sign blazoned the name, CONTINENTAL COURT, against the star-scattered sky, and Duke Morey said: "Let's pull in here a minute, Tom." It was an elaborate California-style auto court, with a line of gasoline pumps and two lunch stands out front. The main building consisted of a central lobby, with a restaurant on the left, a bar in the right wing. The kitchen was at the rear, and employee living quarters occupied the second floor. In the background were row on row of trim handsome cabins, well-spaced for privacy on shrub-bordered lawns, with automobiles parked in the drives.

Tom Garrick eased the convertible to a halt in the gravel yard, and they sat there for a moment, watching the gaudy colored lights and listening to the blare of juke-box music and the rise and fall of laughter and many voices. "A gold mine," Spider Pratt said. "I always told Mr. Ellinger he oughta open a layout like this."

Duke Morey lit a cigarette and looked at Garrick. "What do you think of taking a cabin here, Tom? We'll have Spider phone Ellinger and get them out here—if they'll come."

"It might come off, Duke. We can give it a play, if you want to."

"Who's Ellinger got left?"

"Well, he's lost all his top gunmen, except Zolnay and Kern—and maybe Rudy Valance."

"We could take them, Tom."

"We could try like hell," Garrick said calmly.

"They're all filled up, them cabins," Spider Pratt protested.

"We'll soon find out about that," said Duke Morey, getting out of the car and limbering his left leg with experimental care. "I'll see what they've got, Tom." He hobbled away toward the main entrance.

Garrick nodded and drew the cork from the bottle of scotch. Spider Pratt shook his head and bit a chew off a plug of tobacco. "I been dry for seventeen years, Mr. Tom. Eighteen come next St. Patrick's Day."

In the lobby, Duke discovered there was a vacant cabin at the far end of the last row, Number 100, which was ideal for their purposes. He paid in advance, accepted the key and directions, and returned to the car. Garrick drove through to the back row and turned to the right, parking beside Number 100 at the end of the line. Only a few of the bungalows were still lighted and awake, at this late hour, and none of them were in this area.

Duke unlocked the door and switched on the lights, followed by Pratt and then Garrick, carrying the two bottles. "Very cosy," Duke said, closing the venetian blinds on all the windows and exploring the clean well-furnished place. There was a comfortable living-room, with two bedrooms opening on the left, a shining white modern bathroom with shower between them. At the rear was a neat little kitchen, complete with electric stove, refrigerator, sink, utensils and dishes and glasses. "A nice setup," Duke said, and picked up the telephone, while Garrick poured drinks and Spider Pratt chewed his tobacco morosely.

"No wonder sin flourishes, with places like this all over the country," Tom Garrick remarked. "No wonder there's so much shacking-up done, Spider."

"I wouldn't know about that, Mr. Tom," said Spider primly.

"You mean you renounced sex as well as drinking, Spider?"

"I live clean," Spider said, with dignity. "Like Mr. Ellinger."

Duke Morey called the Twenty-fifth Precinct, identified himself, and learned with vast relief that Jane Tolman was safe and unhurt, found by the police in Number 233 at the Fenwick Apartments. They had also discovered the chauffeur's body in the alley, and taken into custody three members of Ellinger's follow-up crew, apprehended in Number 221. Ellinger's headquarters was surrounded, but his whereabouts were unknown ... Duke advised them to keep a loose cordon around the brownstone building. If the cops closed in, they'd lose the big ones, because there were several secret escapes from the agency. Duke also told them about his plan to lure Ellinger and his associates out to Continental Court, Cabin 100, and requested police cover for that operation.

The desk sergeant promised adequate support, and said that the FBI was cooperating with them in this matter. It looked like the breaking of a case, that the federal investigators had been working on for a long time ... Duke thanked him and hung up, weak with relief. Things were looking better for their cause. He and Tom might even be cited for valor, instead of charged with murder.

After a careful rehearsal, they put the reluctant trembling Spider Pratt on the phone to call Horace Ellinger at his unlisted office number, covering him casually with their guns. The boss was there, and Spider seemed on the verge of fainting, but he went through with it:

"We got 'em, Mr. Ellinger, we got Tom Garrick and Duke Morey ... Out here at Continental Court, Number One Hundred ... Mr. Desmond and Mr. Lomax and Miss Stella Leeds and me, in Stella's car ... No, we can't bring 'em in there, Mr. Ellinger, it's lousy with cops and federal agents ... They got you all penned in, we ain't got a chance to get through to you ... You better come out here, Mr. Ellinger, if you can make it. There's coppers all around you ...

"No, they're busy workin' over the prisoners right now, they told me to call you ... No, she can't, Miss Stella's in the bathroom... Yeah, yeah, sure... We'll hold 'em and wait for you, Mr. Ellinger... Yes sir, Mr. Ellinger... All right, Mr. Ellinger... One Hundred Continental Court, right on the road out to the Chateau... We'll hang on and wait." Spider Pratt, pale and sweating, hung up the telephone with a shaky hand and glared balefully at Duke and Garrick. "I hadn't oughta done that to Mr. Ellinger. I shoulda let you kill me first. I can't never face Mr. Ellinger again."

"Don't worry about it, Spider," said Duke Morey. "Mr. Ellinger will be facing the chair, or a couple hundred years in the pen. If he lives through the night."

They settled down to wait, Duke and Garrick toying with their highball glasses, Spider Pratt sick and miserable over his forced betrayal of a beloved master. Duke Morey switched on the small radio, in the midst of a news broadcast:

"*... And exposure of a great vice ring may be imminent... The chauffeur found dead in an alley beside the Fenwick Apartments on Madison Avenue, has been identified as Herbert Watkins, forty-three, employed by Horace Ellinger, of the Ellinger Escort Service. The two young men, Payton Frappier and Clyde Vorse, who were shot to death in a previously described gun battle, were also in the employ of that Escort Service. Authorities attribute this outbreak of killings to either a gang war, or a revolution within a vice ring.*

"*Here's a flash that just came in. The body of a man found in the harbor last evening has been tentatively identified as that of Anthony J. Castelli, twenty-eight, who was known as Horace Ellinger's personal bodyguard and suspected as a narcotics agent. Badly decomposed from long immersion in the water, there were bullet wounds in the torso and legs of the corpse. There is obviously a link connecting all these underworld slayings. Arrests have been made, and police promise more to follow shortly... Horace Ellinger, Rufus Kern and Benjamin Zolnay, three ranking officials of the Ellinger Escort Service, are still being sought for questioning by the city police and the FBI ... Stand by for further developments in this gangland warfare ... Meanwhile some more recorded music to pass away the wee small hours of very early morning."*

The slow mournful strains of a tune filled the room, and Duke Morey remembered dancing to it with Ann Norvill.

"Maybe we're in after all, Duke," mused Tom Garrick. "Maybe the law's with us instead of agin us, boy."

"Thanks to Jane Tolman and Lolly Durand," said Duke.

"I don't get that radio stuff," Spider Pratt grumbled plaintively. "What they tryin' to frame a man like Horace Ellinger for anyway? What's all this about vice and gang wars and killin's? Mr. Ellinger ain't to blame 'cause you young punks go 'round shootin' each other, is he? Seems like all our trouble begun since you came in with us, Mr. Duke. Could be you're some kinda spy or somethin'."

"Could be, Spider," agreed Duke Morey, admiring the clear amber liquor against the lamplight, and thinking of Ann Norvill with a hollow sense of desolation and loneliness and despair, then thinking of Jane Tolman for a second with guilty excitement.

It was a long dreary wait in Cabin 100, enlivened but little by the slow drinking and chain smoking, the music and late news bulletins of the radio.

"When they come, Spider, you answer the door and let them in," Duke instructed. "Don't try to warn them, or you'll get it right between the shoulders. If they start reaching you hit the deck fast."

"You goin' to kill 'em here? Ain't you killed enough for one night?"

"We won't shoot unless we have to, Spider."

"They may be suspicious and scout the joint first, Duke," suggested Garrick.

"Stella's car ought to convince them, Tom," said Duke Morey. "The blinds are tight on all the windows anyway, and we'll turn the lights down. They won't be able to see inside here. How many you figure will come?"

"The Big Three anyway. Perhaps Valance, if he wasn't hurt bad. That's about all the fighting force Horace has got left."

They turned off the radio and waited in the dimmed-out room, Duke and Garrick nursing drinks and rechecking their guns. They had two weapons apiece. Duke was armed with the .45 he had taken from Tom and the .38 Jane had given him. Garrick had Lomax's Luger and the pistol he had secured from Rudy Valance. Watching them morbidly, Spider Pratt sat munching his tobacco. He never had to spit, and Duke wondered how the little guy could swallow all that juice.

It was 3:35 when the bell rang, startling them all, and Spider moved unhappily toward the door, while Duke and Garrick waited on either side of the short dark entryway, back out of sight with guns held in readiness. Spider opened the door carefully. There was only one man there, a white-jacketed porter carrying a covered tray.

"Your order for Cabin One Hundred, sir," he said.

"We didn't order nothin'," Spider Pratt said.

"But the lady phoned in, sir."

"There ain't no lady here," Spider said. "You got your numbers mixed, bud."

"But I'm certain it was One Hundred," the waiter insisted. "A lady ordering for six persons."

"Naw, there's only three of us here," Spider told him. "Sorry, but we didn't call for nothin'."

"Well, I'm very sorry to disturb you, sir."

"Forget it," Spider Pratt said, shutting and locking the door.

Duke Morey and Tom Garrick looked at one another and shook their heads. Duke said: "Something phoney about that."

"Afraid so, Duke. I don't like it. Somebody sent that guy out here."

Duke nodded. "To check on the lady, and how many were in here. And Spider gave them all the answers... We'd better get down on the floor, Tom. It won't take Ellinger long to figure out the situation. They won't take any chances. They'll spray this shack with machine-gun fire." He studied the interior, searching for the safest places to seek cover.

"Mr. Ellinger knows I'm in here," Spider Pratt said. "He won't let nobody start shootin' with me inside here."

"I wouldn't count too much on that, Spider," advised Duke Morey. "You'd better flatten out somewhere with the rest of us. Four tommy guns can do an awful job on this shanty."

"They won't open fire on me," Spider declared. "Mr. Ellinger thinks too much of me. He says I'm the handiest man he ever had around him."

"Get down, you damn fool!" Tom Garrick said impatiently. "You want to get cut to pieces, Spider?"

"You boys crawl, if you want to," Spider Pratt said stubbornly. "I know what I'm doin'. I don't have to belly down for nobody. Not with Mr. Ellinger comin'. I know Mr. Ellinger, see? He ain't lettin' nobody hurt Spider."

Flattened out against the baseboards in the dimness, Duke Morey and Tom Garrick waited on the floor with guns in either hand, knowing they'd be pinned down and helpless, unable to fire back, if Ellinger and his men ringed the cabin and turned loose their Thompson guns... But Spider Pratt stayed on his feet, pacing back and forth in the living-room, a thin warped little figure with a wrinkled tobacco lumped face.

"That damned Ellinger thinks of all the angles," Duke said. "You'd think Spider's phone call and Stella's convertible would have been enough, but he has to bribe a waiter to come out here and case the joint for him."

"He's a smart sonofabitch," said Garrick.

Spider Pratt turned on him, bristling with indignation. "Don't be talkin' like that about Mr. Ellinger now!"

Tom Garrick grinned. "No offense meant, Spider. Just a manner of speaking. A compliment really."

"He's smart, but he ain't no sonofabitch."

"Granted, Spider, granted. I apologize. Sit down somewhere, Spider, you're making me nervous."

"You oughta be nervous," Spider Pratt said. "You ain't got much of a chance with Mr. Ellinger and Mr. Kern and Mr. Zolnay comin' after you. If I was you I'd be sayin' my prayers."

Tom Garrick laughed softly. "I prayed myself out in a P-38, Spider. I doubt if there's a prayer left in me."

Duke Morey smiled understandingly. "I used up most of mine on the road back to Hungnam. But if it gets bad enough here, I'll probably dig up another one."

"There's always one more left in a man, I guess," Garrick said. "When things get too rough."

Duke inclined his cropped head and tried to relax on the hardwood. He was very tired, his eyes burning heavily and the old wound aching in his left leg, mouth and throat parched dry from too many cigarettes and drinks. He lay there waiting for a sudden shocking blast of machinegun fire to slash the windows and venetian blinds, and rip through walls and tear the ceilings and floors. The fear in him was dulled by extreme weariness. He didn't want to die, although there didn't seem to be a great deal left to live for. There was no panic in him. He felt that what was going to happen would happen as it was written. War makes a fatalist of any thinking man, and Duke Morey was no exception.

CHAPTER TWENTY

The bed creaked as Ann Norvill rose from it and strode to the windows and stared out over the smoky industrial flats, sweltering under the August sunshine in the late afternoon. Her nerves were flayed raw and jittering, her brain raced in senseless circles, and muscles twitched and quivered in her arms and legs. Grayness shrouded her mind like a steaming mist, and that perpetual nausea coiled in the pit of her stomach. Flies buzzed at the window-screens with a drowsy droning summer sound. She tried to remember golden sandy beaches and cool pure water, the exultance of diving and the clean thrill of swimming, but the memories were vague and elusive, part of another lifetime, a different world.

Ann Norvill turned from the bright windows back into the musky closeness of the room, untidy and cluttered as usual, because Peggy had a disorderly mind and Ann no longer cared. At least it was their own bedroom with twin beds, and not a working room such as some of the girls had to sleep in. That was something Ann had insisted on, but even that held small satisfaction now. She had lost track of time here, lost touch with the world and reality... She lit a cigarette, poured three fingers of gin into a glass, and slumped down in the chair before the cheap littered dressing table.

Was that Ann Norvill she saw in the powder-smeared mirror? Ann Norvill, the toast of Cleveland society, the belle of Shaker Heights, the queen of the Vassar campus? ... Her chestnut hair had dulled into drabness, lost its rich gleaming luster, and her blue eyes were faded, sunken and shadowed. Her face looked a trifle bloated, the fine patrician features blurred and coarsened, the mouth slack and loose, the chin slightly sagging. She looked sick and old, soiled and tainted, bewildered and hurt and broken. Her figure, the full flowing curves revealed by the filmy negligee, was still superb, but no longer a delight to her. It had been abused and maltreated too long, by how many hundreds or thousands of male brutes? She saw no more beauty in it, felt it to be just so much defiled and dirtied flesh.

She swallowed the gin, inhaled deeply on the cigarette, and poured another and larger drink. It didn't do much for her any more. It took dope to give her a lift nowadays. That was the only kick left for her, all that she really lived for and craved. And it kept her in this brothel, of course, close to the steady source of drugs, as the vice lords had planned it.

Peggy didn't mind this life. She rather liked it, in fact, for she had far more clothes and perfumes and furs and jewels than she'd ever dreamed of possessing. "When these jerks ask me how I got into this business, I tell 'em I'm a natural—a natural born whore," Peggy said, laughing merrily. "What the hell, it's true. At eleven my step-father copped my cherry, just like in the old sob-story books. At thirteen they caught me in the lumberyard with half the boys in grammar school takin' turns on me. At fifteen I was layin' most of the guys in high school and one of the teachers and a few of the local business men. Why hell, I gave away millions of bucks worth of it, before I smartened up! Who says it ain't a good racket, to get paid for doin' somethin' you like to do?"

But this life was killing Ann Norvill, had killed her already. She felt like an empty corroded shell, drifting through an endless nightmare existence, without aim or direction, point or meaning. There were times when she hovered on the brink of the black bottomless abyss of madness, and mornings that she woke up screaming silently from atrocious dreams of insanity, unendurable torture and terror. Only heroin capsules or cocaine-needles could ease and soothe her.

Ann Norvill wanted to die. She had been longing for death for some time, but more than ever since Lolly Durand had appeared here, a blonde spectre from the past, and told Ann that Duke Morey was back from the war and hunting for her. Then Lolly had run away somehow, vanished from 1260 Brushwood, and Ann feared that Lolly would tell Duke where she was, and he'd come after her … She couldn't let Duke see her like this, a whore in a cheap whorehouse. She'd rather die, die a hundred deaths, than to have Duke find her here. Death was her one salvation, the single way out of this sordid mess.

Ann wondered at the initiative and enterprise, the daring audacity of Lolly Durand in escaping from this bordello-prison. Lolly, whom Ann had always regarded as a frivolous, shallow, flutter-brained nonentity … Why hadn't *she,* Ann Norvill, broken away before it was too late?

But for herself, Ann realized dimly, it was too late when she first came here. Far too late, after Gene Desmond and Park Lomax and the others had finished with her. Ill and shuddering, gagging on the raw gin and cigarette smoke, Ann Norvill recalled the horror of that first night, waking from a drugged stupor to find herself in bed between Desmond and Lomax, to discover what had happened to her. After they'd had enough of her, they turned her over to Payton Frappier and Clyde Vorse, and that was even worse. But in the final hideous round with Tony Castelli and Frank Borchek, she had really been dragged to the bottom-most depths of obscenity and depravity. There was no hope at all for her, after that degrading experience. Ann Norvill was lost, dead to the world of normal decent living, gone forever from Duke Morey.

Why hadn't she given herself to Duke, before he went away? They had both wanted it and needed it, their unconsummated love-making agonizing at times … That would have been something, she'd at least have that to remember and hold onto. But no, they'd decided to wait, painful as it was, and to be married when Duke returned from war—if he did return. *We took a long chance, and we lost,* Ann Norvill thought, grief and anguish welling up within her. *Duke lived through it and came back. I'm the one that died, a victim of the home front.*

She tried to recall exactly the way Duke Morey looked, so tall and strong, smooth and graceful, with his short sandy hair and clear gray eyes, his strong-boned features and wide boyish smile, a slight dimple in one bronzed cheek, a twinkle in his glance. Clean-looking and easy-moving, always well-groomed and wearing his clothes with a casual flair. Cleaner looking than anyone else, Ann Norvill thought, scrubbed outside and shining with some sort of inner cleanness too, big and rangy, quiet and pleasant. She remembered his laughter, and his soft gentle voice.

Several years before they met in Manhattan, Ann Norvill had seen Duke Morey play basketball and baseball in Columbus, when Wisconsin visited Ohio State, and one night she had danced with him at the SAE House, and that first flare of feeling had sprung up between them even then. Duke didn't know she had read somewhere that he was an SAE, and so had made it a point to date an Ohio member of the fraternity that night, in hopes of meeting Duke Morey at the party. He'd never know it now ... It was all over, ended before it was really begun, a broken dream and a closed book.

She only hoped he'd never show up at 1260 Brushwood. Since Lolly had made her getaway, Ann Norvill lived in mortal dread of finding Duke downstairs among the customers some evening. Sooner or later it was bound to happen, Duke was sure to come after her ... Death was the only way to avoid that meeting, and death it would be. An overdose of sleeping pills was the simplest way out. Ann poured some more gin, and searched the dresser drawers for the capsules, but they seemed to be gone. Well, some of the girls would have a supply of them. Ann must remember to inquire tonight. A compulsion for haste was on her, all at once. Duke Morey would be coming before long. She could feel it all through her. She loved and wanted him more than ever, but she couldn't let him catch her in this brothel. Much better if he found her in the morgue.

Ann Norvill paced the floor, glass in hand, looking out at the bleak manufacturing town, with the lowering sun setting fire to the westward facing windows and giving the sooty haze a ruddy tinge above the rooftops. Across the corridor a record-player was grinding out a bawdy song and girlish laughter rose shrill and loud. Ann wondered how they could laugh about sex, when they trafficked in it every night of their lives. Down the hall another highly different record was playing, and groping back in her fogged mind Ann thought it was Paderewski playing Rachmaninoff's *Prelude in C Sharp Minor.*

Twilight was at the windows and Ann Norvill was stretched in sodden hopelessness on her bed, when the door finally opened and Peggy came in with a breezy strut, bleached hair shining like brass and rouged face smiling cheerily. She was showily attired for the street, her ripe body swelling the sharp lines of the white gabardine suit, a scarlet bow at her throat matching the bag under her arm and the high-heeled ankle-strapped red shoes on her feet.

"You still mopin' 'round here, honey?" said Peggy. "You oughta get out more, kid. It's no good layin' in the sack all day, baby."

"I'm tired," Ann Norvill said. "I'm always tired."

"You drink too much gin, dearie. Get cleaned up and we'll go down and eat."

"I'm not hungry."

"You got to eat. A girl can't work if she don't eat. Snap out of it, Ann."

"I'm not working tonight," Ann Norvill said. "I'm sick."

Peggy laughed. "There's only two kinds of sickness gets you out of workin' here, hon. The curse or a dose, you know that. And you ain't got neither right now, sweet. Get up and make yourself beautiful."

"The hell with it. I'm all through, Peg. I'll never take on another crummy customer in this filthy house."

"Knock it off, kid," said Peggy. "You know damn well you can't get away with that. You want them pimps in here beatin' your brains out? Listen, sweetie pie, I got you out of one stinkin' job tonight. Lady Macbeth was goin' to send you out to put on an act as a stag party with four-five other girls. I told her you wouldn't buy that and finally talked her out of it. You know what that woulda meant, don't you, dear? Daisy chain stuff in front of a few hundred men, and not the kinda daisy chains you used to have at Vassar!"

"Lady Macbeth," mused Ann Norvill, rather proud of the title she had bestowed upon the hard-faced flint-hearted Madam of the establishment. "Tell her I've got to have a shot, if I'm going to work tonight. None of those heroin capsules either. Tell her to bring the needle, the real junk."

Peggy shook her brassy head, worriment on her bold handsome face. "You ain't goin' to last long, baby, if you don't lay off that junk."

"Who cares?" Ann said. "Who wants to last long here?"

"Me, for one," said Peggy. "Maybe this ain't Park Avenue, but it's a helluva lot better than a hole in the ground, darlin'. I'll stick around for a while longer."

"Go call Lady Macbeth, Peggy," said Ann wearily.

"I ain't your Girl Friday neither, princess!"

"Please, Peg. I'm sick, really sick."

"You're soft," Peggy said, with contempt. "All you rich bitches are soft like that. You go to hell a lot quicker'n us peasants."

Ann Norvill sighed. "How stupid can you get?"

"You're callin' *me* stupid?" Peggy yelled. "I oughta bat your ears off! You're the stupid one, sister, rum dumb and coked-up all the time. You been whorin' a year and you're all washed up. I been whorin' all my life and I'm good for twenty-thirty years more."

"All right, Peggy," said Ann. "I'll concede the point. You're a better whore than I am. Now will you please call Lady Macbeth?"

Peggy groaned and gestured extravagantly. "Sure, sure, anythin' for the aristocracy! Your servant, Mrs. Dupont. I'll call your keeper."

Madam entered fifteen minutes later, large and statuesque with a face of rough-hewn rock and eyes like ice. Holding a syringe in her hand, she frowned solemnly down at the girl on the bed. "You're going to end up taking the cure, if you keep this up, Ann. You upper crust dames aren't worth a damn in this business anyway. I keep telling them to pick up the good tough ones out of the gutter, and to hell with you fine young ladies."

"Is that a real good shot?" Ann Norvill asked.

"It's enough for a horse or two. You're getting to be a lot more expensive than you're worth here. Take a bath and get fixed up nice now. Most of the mills paid off today, and we're going to have a big night." She applied the syringe with an expert hand.

"Oh, God," moaned Ann.

"You'll be okay when that takes hold, babe. Come down and eat when you're ready, and stay off that gin bottle. We got some nice roast beef tonight."

Ann nodded mechanically, almost retching at the mention of food. "I haven't been sleeping well. Got to get some nembutal or sodium amytal or something."

Lady Macbeth grimaced. "You society dames sure get all the good habits, don't you? I'll get you some pills when you're through work. Don't be taking too many of the damn things though. All we need in here is a corpse, with all the heat they got on us."

"I'll be careful." Ann Norvill smiled up at her, beginning to feel better already. "I've got a lot to live for, you know."

"Yeah, we all have. But sometimes I wonder what the hell it is."

"If you see a tall fine-looking young man with light-brown crewcut hair and gray eyes and a sweet smile," Ann said dreamily. "Don't let him in here."

"Christ, you got a jag already?" said Madam, disgusted. "Who pays any attention to what they look like? After a while they're like Chinese, they all look the same. Haven't you noticed that? If he's that good, what'd he be coming here for anyway?"

"He might be looking for me, Lady Macbeth," said Ann, smiling remotely.

"I knew you'd bring trouble sometime, you little slut!" Madam slapped her face with a heavy hand. "All I know is you hung that name on me, but don't be calling me that to my face, see? I'll knock your teeth right down your throat, if you ever call me that again! Now get yourself cleaned up and organized, and get downstairs. You aren't a privileged character around here."

Still smiling, in spite of her bruised and reddened cheek, Ann Norvill watched the stately departure of the big rawboned woman. Then she rose from the bed with new buoyancy, life flowing once more in her veins. Even the prospect of entertaining thirty or forty half-drunken millhands no longer daunted her. Why should it? That was her trade, the only one she had ever mastered. And on the whole, drunk or sober, they were more gentlemanly and decent than Ellinger's Escorts had been ....

When the evening rush started, Ann Norvill was in the reception line with the rest of the scantily clad girls, wearing a sheer evening gown with nothing underneath it, smiling and flushed and fairly blooming now, alive and desirable and beyond caring about anything once more... "Come on, big boy. You never been loved, until you been loved by Annie!"

"She from Shaker Heights," crooned Bertha, the high-yellow. "'She can sure shake that thing, oh mister man! That little old gal from Shaker Heights, she shakes that thing like nobody else! ... But Bertha here's blazin' tonight, menfolks! Bertha, she takes you to New Orleans, Paris, all over Europe, clear round the world!"

Sometime, somewhere, during that long hectic night in 1260 Brushwood, Ann Norvill chanced to catch some familiar names in a radio newscast, and learned that Clyde Vorse and Payton Frappier had been shot to death in a street fight in midtown New York, and Tony Castelli's body had been fished out of the harbor. She was glad they were dead, actually *glad,* and she hoped that Desmond and Lomax and Borchek would get it too. All the men who had first violated her.

Ann had a feeling that Darnell Duke Morey was involved somehow, and perhaps had done the killing himself, or taken some part in it. She sensed that Duke was taking his revenge for what they had done to her, and also that he was in grave danger tonight. She prayed briefly and earnestly for his life and welfare and future happiness.

And she was more afraid than ever that Duke would be coming here in search of her. She thought these things as she looked up into the nameless face of one of thousands of men she had known—but never really known—since she came here. She felt these things as—and it happened every so often—a crude, animal pleasure ran through her body, a hard pleasure that lifted her up even better than the dope for a moment, that made her hips momentarily drumbeat under the man she was with, made her breasts tingle and her thighs quiver for a few seconds, but then dropped her down even further into the depths than she had been before, as the pleasure slowly subsided within her, and she hated it for what it could have been—for what it never was—with Darnell Duke Morey.

CHAPTER TWENTY-ONE

Jane Tolman, recovered from the knockout drops but, still dazed and groggy, sat in the back seat of a Twenty-fifth Precinct squad car beside Lolly Durand, one of many police cars rushing out past the Park and through Harlem and the Bronx, in the early morning darkness. The radio in front buzzed with a steady frying sound, with voices breaking through now and then. Some of the neon signs they passed intensified the static to a screeching pitch, and the subsequent softer hum was a relief when the tubular lights were left behind.

Patrolman Joe Flynn, a lean, wiry, red-faced, dark-haired young man was at the wheel, pushing the sedan along with skilled speed. Beside him sat Patrolman Dan Carrigan, a broad solid bulk of a man, with a square-jawed harsh-lined face, mild tired eyes, and thinning gray hair under his cap. On the dash in front of Carrigan, a tiny green bulb lighted whenever a call flashed on the air waves.

Lolly Durand had been with them for hours, and felt as if she had known them all her life. She had waited with them outside the Parkmont on Central Park West earlier in the evening, and raced with them over to the Fenwick on Madison when the emergency call came through. Lolly had been in the car, when Carrigan and Flynn and the other cops found Jane Tolman unconscious in Number 233 and arrested three men in Number 221, and come upon the body of Chauffeur Herbert Watkins in the alley beside the apartment house. Jane had come to, sooner than expected, refusing to go in the ambulance, preferring to join Lolly in this patrol car.

After Jane was fully revived at the station, Car 814 had become part of the mobile cordon looped about Ellinger's brownstone headquarters building, and they were cruising in that district when Duke Morey's last phone call reached the Two-Five Precinct.

Horace Ellinger and three companions—believed to be Kern and Zolnay and Valance—had slipped through the loose cordon of police, emerging some distance away from the escort bureau and driving off in a big maroon car with a souped-up motor. They had been spotted, however, and the law was in full chase now, speeding along various routes toward Continental Court on the northern outskirts.

Crouched in the rear of Car 814, Jane Tolman thought of Duke Morey and Tom Garrick, waiting out there in a dark cabin, the bait that was to trap Ellinger and his chieftains. The bait that might be sacrificed, before the cops could close in. Jane knew that she loved Duke Morey, had loved him for a long time, striving to hide and suppress it because of her loyalty to Ann Norvill. She had thought her love was hopeless, that Duke wasn't going to forget Ann, or get over her loss. Now maybe all that was changed.

"You must've been awful scared, Jane," said Lolly Durand.

Jane just nodded.

The green bulb glowed on the dashboard and another call came in, the crackling jumbled words unintelligible in the back seat of the sedan. When the message ended, Dan Carrigan turned his rugged face and said: "The FBI broke into the Chateau, Ellinger's estate up the Hudson. Found three more dead there. Desmond and Lomax and a woman named Stella Leeds, all Ellinger employees. Your boy-friend is having a night for himself, girls."

"You think he—Duke Morey—did it?" Jane Tolman asked.

"Who else?"

"Tom Garrick must be with him. You think they killed Vorse and Frappier and that chauffeur too?"

"It figures," Carrigan said. "And it looks as if all they need is time enough to wipe out the whole bunch."

"They must be good," Joe Flynn said. "But not that good, Dan. Ellinger's crew is loaded with sub-machine guns, they say. Automatics aren't much good against them."

"Tom Garrick's awful good-looking too," Lolly Durand said, irrelevantly. "Not as nice as Duke, but real distinguished."

Jane Tolman gestured impatiently. "Will there be charges? Against Duke Morey and Tom Garrick?"

"If this case is what it looks like, Miss Tolman, there'll be medals and bonuses and headlines for them two boys." Carrigan smiled back at the girls. "The FBI found a secret vault in the Chateau, crammed with files and records that will probably establish Horace Ellinger as head of a nationwide vice organization. So your boys are doing all right—even though they're chiseling in on police work."

"They couldn't do it any other way," Jane Tolman said. "You know the law never would touch Ellinger before."

Dan Carrigan nodded, scowling. "I hate to admit it, lady, but you got something there, I guess. Ellinger always swung a lot of weight around in high places."

Joe Flynn pulled out and streaked past a couple of cars with the horn screaming angrily, and the veteran Carrigan subsided into silence, aware that young Joe thought he was talking too much. They roared on through the night, racing against time, with intermittent reports flashing in on the progress of the Ellinger vehicle. It was still well ahead of the pack, apparently, and gaining constantly with that hopped-up power under the maroon hood. It was fortunate that the police knew Ellinger's destination in advance, or the pursuit might have been futile.

"This Morey boy was in Korea?" inquired Joe Flynn. "Must be hell over there."

"I guess it was," Jane said. "He never talked much about it."

"And Garrick?"

"He flew a P-38 in the last war."

Joe Flynn nodded gravely. "They both been there then. They know the score all right. I was a waist-gunner in a B-26 over Germany."

"Don't get me started talking about the first war, Joe," said Dan Carrigan, with a chuckle.

"A picnic," the driver needled, grinning. "A vacation in Paris."

"It didn't seem that way in the Argonne," Carrigan said mildly.

"Popguns and pea-shooters," laughed Flynn, and Jane Tolman knew it was an old argument with them, a game they often played to while away the long hours on patrol. They were playing it now, a little self-conscious and awkward, to take the girls' minds off the situation at hand, the dangerous spot that Duke Morey and Tom Garrick were in.

Two men armed only with pistols, holed up in a tourist cabin, waiting for four desperate criminals carrying murderous machine guns. Unless Duke and Tom could surprise Ellinger's crew, their chances were slim and small.

An FBI car called in from above the auto court, reporting no sign of the maroon-colored sedan up there as yet. Ellinger and his men must have arrived at the Continental.

"Can't we go any faster, Joe?" asked Jane Tolman, beseechingly.

"Sorry, ma'am," Joe Flynn said. "This crate's wide open. But there are other patrol cars ahead of us. They can't be too far behind Ellinger."

"I know ... I ought to keep my mouth shut."

"You talk all you want to, little girl," Dan Carrigan said gruffly.

Lolly Durand reached over and pressed Jane's hand. "They'll be okay, Janie. Those two guys can take care of themselves but good."

"Oh, God, I hope so!" Jane Tolman murmured, sighing.

"You go for that Duke, don't you?"

Jane nodded slowly.

At last the lofty orange-and-blue conflagration of the Continental Court sign loomed ahead of them, and Car 814 finally swerved into the large parking area, that was already lined with police cars and motor bikes, and swarming with uniformed coppers and state troopers and plain-clothes men.

Joe Flynn eased along to the far end of the lot and turned into the perimeter driveway, and Dan Carrigan cradled the riot gun in his broad lap. The rows of cabins stretched away into the darkness, and behind them rose a steep rocky height of land, broken by the large crescent indentation of an old gravel pit. Joe cut his lights and inched the car forward. The maroon sedan was nowhere in view.

Jane Tolman, hands clenched tensely and panic fluttering in her breast, was praying in breathless silence, when the first vicious chatter of machine-gun fire burst out and rose into a shattering roar, the flames lighting the far back corner of the great rectangle of neat spaced bungalows.

Joe Flynn turned into shelter between the first and second rows of cabins, and the two officers got out. "You girls stay in the car and keep down low," Dan Carrigan said calmly. "This hadn't oughta take too long."

Jane Tolman shivered with a chill that bit bone-deep. Nobody could possibly live through gunfire like that. She could see Duke Morey and Tom Garrick shot to pieces, riddled and sprawling, dead in their own blood.

CHAPTER TWENTY-TWO

Waiting in Cabin 100, Duke Morey and Tom Garrick had barricaded themselves with furniture and mattresses on the floor, but Spider Pratt refused to get down under cover. Duke knew now that they should have waited outside for the enemy, but it was too late to correct an error in tactics after that waiter came. Outside they could have flanked and surprised the Ellinger outfit perhaps. Trapped inside they were virtually helpless, sitting ducks, targets in a shooting gallery.

The firing started with the sound of bursting boilers and steampipes, machine guns raking the structure fore and aft with wicked bursts. The first blast stitched Spider Pratt across the middle and all but cut him in half, flinging him back on the wall like a rag-doll, dropping him in a welter of blood as he rebounded to midfloor. Broken glass and fragments of metal venetian blinds showered the interior, splinters and mortar raining down on Duke and Tom, as they flattened out hugging the hardwood.

Cross-whipping streams of fire snarled and crackled, splintering furniture, scoring walls and ceilings, searing through the mattresses, close enough to tug at the clothing and scorch the flesh of the two men on the floor. The radio, lamps, bottles and glasses exploded. A choking haze of plaster and cordite filled the air, illuminated by lightning-like gun flames. Pictures were snatched from the walls. Glassware and pottery shattered to pieces in the kitchen. Bullets burst mirrors and shredded woodwork and whanged off metal. The torn body of Spider jerked from the jolting impacts, and the carpet was ripped to ribbons.

Duke Morey had been praying, silently and automatically, but he gave it up. There was no chance of surviving here. He thought Garrick was dead, and couldn't understand how he himself had lasted this long. Torrents of lead slammed furniture against him and punched through mattresses and searched every corner. The cabin was a riddled reeking inferno, clouded with firelit smoke and dust and powdered mortar.

Suddenly the guns stopped. The men outside knew that no one could be left alive on the interior. Duke Morey raised his head and watched the ruined front door and the wrecked windows, waiting for a target, the silence a strange and awesome thing after that deafening racket. But nobody came, nothing moved except the swirling smoke. Ellinger and his men were so sure they weren't going to bother to investigate. They were pulling out, and the police would be too late.

Duke turned to look at Garrick's body, and his heart went up in glad surprise. Tom was alive, grinning at him through a mask of grime and dust. "I found another prayer, Duke," he said.

"I found a hundred of 'em, Tom," said Duke Morey, and started crawling toward the windows where broken twisted venetian blinds hung raggedly against jagged shards of glass....

Outside, Horace Ellinger said: "Give them one more burst and we'll travel."

Kern and Zolnay and Valance lined their tommy guns and turned loose a final blast at the bungalow. Once more the silence was eerie and dense after the hammering gunfire. Satisfied, Ellinger turned to lead them back to the maroon sedan, but something brought him up short and peering. A fleeting glimpse of uniformed figures prowling among the cabins that were suddenly alive with lights and panicky questioning voices, the wailing of children and the hysteria of women, the hoarse shouts of men.

"Coppers," Ellinger said calmly. "Back this way. See if the key's in Stella's car. If it isn't we'll have to run for it. Or fort up and fight." His spectacled eyes swept the ridge behind the last row of cabins, as they moved back toward the smoking shambles of Number 100 and the silver convertible parked beside it.

Rufus Kern and Ben Zolnay were covering this brief retreat, pacing backward with guns at the ready, but the police advance was slow and wary. Naturally they didn't want any free-for-all shooting match in this crowded tourist court. Rudy Valance had run ahead to check on Stella Leeds' car. Now he was calling and motioning them on, with happy relief in his tone.

"We can make it," Ellinger said casually. "They can't start shooting among all these cabins."

Valance had already settled behind the wheel, and Ellinger got in beside him while Kern and Zolnay climbed into the rear. "Swing around back," directed Ellinger, indicating the perimeter drive that encircled the entire area of the court....

Within the wreckage of Cabin 100, Duke Morey and Tom Garrick were still flattened out from that last burst when they heard voices and then the sudden uproar of the motor beneath Rudy Valance's foot.

Garrick groaned: "O Christ, I left the key in the car!"

Rising and rushing to the windows, they wrenched at the tangled metal slats of the blinds, but the car was already moving away, its spinning wheels throwing gravel in an abrupt start.

"Out back!" Duke yelled, and ran for the kitchen with Garrick after him, tripping and stumbling over debris and Spider Pratt's body in the darkness. The rear door was bolted. Duke tore at it with frantic fingers and they burst outside. The convertible had already roared past, heading down behind the long line of cabins. They opened fire with their pistols, hitting the dirt when machine-gun fire blazed back at them from the rear seat. With bullets hailing all around and kicking dust in their faces, Duke and Tom kept on triggering from prone positions, hoping to hit the tires or the gas tank.

At the mouth of the gravel pit, the silver car slewed out of control in a billowing dustcloud, as tires blew at high speed and sent it slithering crazily from side to side. There was a terrific rending crash and the screech of tortured crumbling steel, as the convertible piled into a boulder and overturned, spilling occupants in all directions in a storm of flying earth. Duke and Tom were on their feet and running, when flames burst from the wreckage and spread garish light over the scene.

Two of the men on the ground lay motionless and looked dead, and Duke recognized the once-elegant form of Rudy Valance and the frog-like bulk of Horace Ellinger. But the other two, Kern and Zolnay, were conscious and stirring, scrabbling about to recover their submachine guns and get away from the burning vehicle into the shelter of the gravel pit.

Duke had emptied the .45 at the car, and was running now with the .38 swinging in his right hand, dragging his left leg in agony. Tom Garrick was about twenty yards ahead of him with the Luger, and Duke panted out a warning as he saw the lanky figure of Rufus Kern come up in crouching silhouette against the flaming automobile. Kern was stunned, staggering, trying to lift his Thompson into line. The gun began to stutter on a down-slant, chewing up the roadway toward Garrick, and Tom started returning the fire, weaving in his run.

A slug from Garrick's Luger smashed Kern's chest and beat him backward, and the tommy gun jerked up just high enough to reach Garrick and cut him down. Tom fell in a crippled roll, body writhing and legs drawn up.

Ben Zolnay had disappeared into the dark crescent of the gravel pit, and Duke Morey couldn't locate him until the muzzle flashes stabbed out of the blackness and bullets began to eat up gravel in his direction. Beyond all fear and caution now, Duke halted in a balanced crouch and started shooting steadily at the flares from Zolnay's barrel. Dirt was spattering Duke's knees and the clip in the .38 was running out, when the tommy gun tilted a final burst straight down and the squat frame of Ben Zolnay toppled forward over it in the fading muzzle lights.

Duke Morey walked into the pit and found Zolnay dead with his beaked face against a rock. Duke picked up the tommy gun and turned back toward the fiery ruins of the car, and saw the perimeter drive swarming now with uniformed men. There was small group around Tom Garrick, and a larger clump around Ellinger and Valance. A long sigh of weariness broke from Duke's parched lips, and the relief was so great he felt weak and faint from it. On numb slack legs he walked slowly back to the road, and was instantly surrounded by policemen and questions.

But Duke had a query of his own, the uppermost thing in his mind: "How's Tom? Tom Garrick?"

One cop shook his head. And Duke held back hard tears.

Ellinger and Valance were alive and conscious, though, which was a good thing to have somebody left to answer questions and charges. Kern and Zolnay were dead—along with quite a few other characters. Duke didn't notice their irony, any more than he noticed a look akin to awe in some of the tough hard-bitten faces around him. He was too spent, exhausted and battle-shocked.

But what good does all this do Ann Norvill? he thought, with dull bitterness. *It doesn't bring Ann back to me or back to life... But I'm going across the river and get her out of that place and do what I can for her. And the least the cops can do is help me out... If they don't throw us in jail or something, for taking the law in our own hands. There'll be some kind of charges to face all right. But at least Ellinger's outfit is busted, and Tom and I did it.*

The next few hours were so confusing Duke Morey didn't know whether he was a criminal or a hero.

There were reporters and cameramen and flashbulbs popping, along with all the officials and law-enforcement officers, but Duke Morey wasn't very interested. All he cared was that it was over and Jane Tolman was safe, and the men who had ruined Ann Norvill were either dead or in custody.

The police didn't like it and the Federal Bureau of Investigation wasn't altogether happy about the affair. The results were excellent, but the means reflected little credit on either organization. Still they couldn't help extending a certain respect and admiration to Duke and Tom, as they would have to any two men who carried hand guns into combat against machine weapons.

"We just had a lot of luck," Duke Morey said, sick with fatigue and reaction.

There might have been longer nights in Korea, but Duke couldn't remember any particular one.

CHAPTER TWENTY-THREE

Another night and Jane Tolman was once more riding in Car 814, with wiry Joe Flynn at the wheel and stolid Dan Carrigan at his side, but this time it was quite different because Duke Morey sat on her right with an FBI agent named Hollister on her left. She felt tired but happy with her hand nestling in Duke's. They were going across the river to get Ann Norvill and bring her back as a witness in the Ellinger case, which had the entire nation in a turmoil.

Horace Ellinger and Rudy Valance were in a hospital under heavy guard, for there might be attempts to either free them or silence them forever. The press, radio and television, all the news services of the country, were overladen with sensational stories about the breaking of an enormous vice syndicate by two ex-GI's, supported by the city police and the Federal Bureau of Investigation... Nine persons dead in one long bloody night of scattered gun-fighting. The biggest news story since Captain Carlsen and the *Enterprise*.

Although he had slept in snatches throughout the day, Duke Morey was still close to exhaustion and thoroughly fed up with the law-enforcement agencies and the publicity and all things official and bureaucratic. There was small consolation in the fact that he was going at last to Ann Norvill. It would be a strange and bitter homecoming, one that he actually dreaded now. Instead of a sweetheart and prospective bride, he was going to meet a prostitute and drug addict, a girl ruined and lost beyond redemption. That it was not Ann's fault didn't alter her tragic status.

Duke knew that Ann wouldn't want to see him. She had told Lolly Durand as much. And he was reluctant to look upon the shamed broken creature she had become. But he had to try and save her ... In Duke's misery and desolation, the only comforting thing in the world was the warm presence of Jane Tolman beside him. He felt guilty about what he was thinking as he looked at her ample breasts while they sped to Ann.

With the fighting over, the danger passed, fear was stronger in Duke Morey than it had been in that cabin at Continental Court. When he leaned back and shut his eyes the dead rose up to haunt him, as they had in the snatched intervals of sleep that day, and all the scenes of gun-blasted violence unreeled vividly in his strained mind. Castelli and Borchek on the rainswept deck of a ferry. That chauffeur in the alley beside the Fenwick Apartments. Vorse and Frappier on a bright busy street corner. Desmond and Lomax and Stella Leeds in the chrome-and-leather bar at the Chateau ... Spider Pratt In Cabin 100, and Kern and Zolnay out back by the firelit mouth of an old gravel pit. And then Tom—the best buddy a guy ever had. And a helluva fighter.

They swept through Holland Tunnel in a floodtide of cars, and out across the broad industrial flats of nighttime New Jersey, driving toward a certain city and a notorious address, 1260 Brushwood, where a society girl from Shaker Heights and Vassar had been converted into a common whore ... Visions of what Ann Norvill's life must have been like for the past year and a half set Duke's teeth on edge and locked his fists into aching knots, filled him with hopeless fury and hatred. Feeling his tension, Jane Tolman tried to ease and reassure him with the soft pressure of her fingers, her arm and shoulder, silent because she knew words were useless. But the tension was just as great in her. Would she lose her man?

Duke Morey settled back and tried to relax, but the delicate perfume Jane wore could not drive the raw reek of cordite fumes out of his aching head. He watched the endless stream of headlights coming at them on the highway, and heard the swish-swish of passing cars. He wished he had a drink, a lot of drinks, enough to numb his brain and body beyond thought and feeling. He wanted to get drunk alone in a good soundproof hotel room and then sleep for a week. Not see anybody. Except maybe Jane.

The patrol car entered the town and cruised along streets that Ann Norvill might have walked, after she had been an inmate of 1260 Brushwood long enough to gain daytime freedom rights. Observing various establishments as they passed, Duke pictured her lunching in that restaurant, sipping a drink in a corner drug-store, shopping in this store with the fashionable show windows, buying papers and magazines at the sidewalk newsstand. Or had she been confined all the time, at first forcibly and later volun-tarily, as the drug habit grew on her? … His face went hot and his throbbing head reeled with another thought: *Some of these men along the street might have been her customers, buying for a few dollars the lovely body that should have belonged to him.*

Duke glimpsed an illuminated clock-face with the hands at 10:17. Ann would be on duty now. They might have to wait for her to finish with a client, unless the local police decided to raid the joint… He didn't want to go through with it, didn't want to see Ann Norvill at all. This was the end of a long hard quest, but Duke Morey no longer cared about achieving his objective. It could mean only pain and humiliation and sorrow for both of them. He wished he'd never mention her name to the law, and suggested this mission. It was as futile as digging up the casket of someone long dead.

But perhaps she can still be saved and restored, he thought. *If so it is certainly worth a little more suffering on my part. After what Ann has gone through, I should cry over being hurt a bit harder. What the hell's the matter with me anyway? Am I setting myself up as judge and jury, as well as executioner?*

Hollister passed cigarettes around but Duke shook his head, and the quiet FBI man lit Jane's and then his own. Duke needed something a lot stronger than tobacco. Up front Flynn and Carrigan were arguing without heat over the Dodgers and the Giants. It was a sooty squalid factory town they had come to, and Duke contemplated with a shudder of revulsion the types of men that Ann Norvill must have entertained. But, as Lolly Durand had said, they were better than Castelli and Borchek and the rest of Ellinger's Escorts.

Their first stop was the police station in the Brushwood precinct. Carrigan and Hollister got out to confer and make arrangements with the local authorities, leaving the other three in the car.

Joe Flynn turned a hard ruddy profile. "I still say them Yanks knock the Sox right down Chicago's throat."

"They're bad-ball hitters though," Duke said.

Flynn grinned. "So what? So's Yogi Berra but he don't do bad for himself."

"No, Yogi does all right," Duke admitted, thinking: There's always baseball anyway. Thank God for baseball. Without it America would be a sad sorry place... He spotted a ruby neon bar sign down the street, and said: "I need a drink. Join me, Jane?"

"Yes, I wouldn't mind one myself, Duke."

"Don't blame you a bit." Joe Flynn wet his lips wistfully. "Wish I could go along with you."

"Come on," Duke invited. "Glad to have you."

"Thanks but I better stick here. Papa Carrigan might spank. You folks go ahead and take an extra one for me."

It was pleasurable to get out and stretch, but Duke Morey's legs felt weak and lifeless, and the sound of his heels on the walk seemed to come from a distance. They moved slowly through light and shadow, Jane's head barely coming to his sagged shoulder, and all at once he was very grateful to have her with him. It was as if they belonged together, and had come to see an old mutual friend who had fallen in evil ways and become almost a stranger to them. It wasn't fair to Ann Norvill, but that's the way Duke felt.

"I'm afraid, Duke," said Jane Tolman, her hand tightening on his arm. "I don't know why, but I am."

"Nothing to be afraid of—now," Duke said, but the same fear was cold in under his breastbone.

"I wish I hadn't come."

"You had to, Janie. I needed you."

"Then I'm glad I came, Duke." She smiled up at him, with a sudden bright warmth that dazzled his eyes and made something catch hurtingly in his throat.

"It won't be easy—or pleasant."

"Certainly not—for Ann. But if there's a chance ... If there's anything we can do, Duke."

"Yeah, I know," he said. "We'll try and we'll hope, Janie."

It wasn't a bad little bar, with the lighting about right, the bartender and the few customers quiet and pleasant, the gaudy rainbow colors of the inevitable juke box flowing and shifting as the discs revolved and the music came out low and sweet. Duke wondered if Ann had ever dropped in here for a drink or two, Ann with some of the other girls from 1260 Brushwood. Or Ann with some man.

They drank bourbon and soda, and listened idly to the music and the men along the bar discussing the Ellinger case. "Think they'll close this town up? ... They'll button everything up tight—until it blows over ... Heard they knocked off some joints already ... Sure, on Brushwood, they had to ... After they found that ..."

Duke ordered another round, in honor of Patrolman Flynn, and Jane studied him gravely. "You know, Duke, I always remembered something you said once. A long time ago at a party in the Village, at Ann's studio, I think. Somebody said, 'Why you always laughing, Morey?' And you said, 'Because I feel like crying.'"

He nodded, with a slow dim smile. "Sure, Janie. I coined that gem on the campus at Madison."

"Until then I always thought you were gay and reckless and go-to-hell," Jane Tolman mused. "After that I saw the sadness underneath. Have you always been sad, Duke?"

"Well, I've had a lot of fun, Janie—or so it seemed. But I've never been too happy, I guess."

"I'd like to—" she broke off and started again. "I think Ann could have made you happy."

"Maybe." Duke drained his glass. "One more for old Carrigan."

"Not for me, Duke. You have another."

"I'll make it a double to cover Carrigan and Hollister both," he said. "Then we'd better go, I suppose..."

When they got back to the car, Carrigan and Hollister were standing on the sidewalk beside it.

A few minutes later they were at 1260 Brushwood. And a few seconds after that, Duke was standing amidst a group of policemen, who were talking to an ugly looking woman that had to be the head of the house, and then one of the officers was walking up to Duke and saying, "Third floor, Morey. Third door, left side."

And Duke was walking the stairs, alone, like a man walking to his own execution.

CHAPTER TWENTY-FOUR

Duke stood before Ann Norvill. The feeling he felt inside was indescribable. The only ones he had ever known in his life to rival it were the love he once knew for Ann, the excitement he felt for Jane that last night, and the sorrow at Tom Garrick's death. Now he felt a fourth unbearably feeling—pity. And it twisted his insides until they ached.

"Duke!" Ann said, almost in a whisper.

"Yes, Ann," Duke answered. "How are you?" he choked out.

Ann's face showed no movement, but she had to clasp her hands together to keep them from shaking. Here she was, fresh from being violated by another filthy, five buck a lay customer, the strain of his manhood still on her loins, the quiver of her own climax still fresh in her senses, talking to the man who was her sweetheart, who was to marry her and carry her virgin-like into their white marriage bed.

"How do I look, Duke?" she asked.

He stepped toward her a little, but didn't touch her. "I know," he said. "I know. But I've come to get you out of here, Ann. We'll change it. You may not even believe it now, but you can be what you were. You—"

"Don't, Duke. Please," she said. "Just get out. Please."

He turned to go. Then he whirled around again. "No, I'm not getting out," he said. "I'll prove to you that this doesn't have to be your life, Ann. You'll see. You've just forgotten what fresh air is like. You're coming with me."

She looked at him, shock running across her features. "All right," she said. "All right, Duke. Just wait outside for a minute while I get dressed."

He looked at her for a second, smiled, then walked out and closed the door behind him.

Inside, Ann Norvill slipped out of her bathrobe. She stood before her mirror for a second and looked at her naked body. Her breasts were still full, but now they hung down a bit, testimony to the nightly mauling of countless men. Her thighs were bruised. That would go in time, but the look on her face would never go. Nor what she knew inside. What she left. What she was.

She closed her eyes for a second, put her hands on her breasts. Her mind fleeted back through time, and it was Duke's hands on her breasts, on her thighs, but never his body completely with her. Duke... Her mind lurched back to the present. Duke was waiting outside. Waiting to give her a new world, the world that once belonged to her—a bright, shining, clean, world where sex was bright, shining, clean. Ann bit her lip to stop from crying. Then she opened the window next to the bed and jumped.

CHAPTER TWENTY-FIVE

Ann Norvill's parents were contacted and the body was sent back to Ohio. A week later, Duke Morey went to take a look at Tom Garrick's grave. He stood there a minute, just thinking. All the loose ends seemed to be tied together now, but the rough way some of them had been tied, his search for Ann, his life as a forced gigolo, his battle against Ellinger and his boys, and the death of Tom Garrick—these things would never leave his mind. Still, there was life. And Jane.

He turned from Tom's grave and walked back up toward the hill. Jane was waiting there. He put his arm around her. Her womanhood pushed against his lower ribs and he tightened his grip as they started toward the top of the hill again.

THE END

www.ingramcontent.com/pod-product-compliance
Lightning Source LLC
Chambersburg PA
CBHW030256270626
47156CB00022B/2799